DON'T MES!

Nate girded himself to move. If he could spring fast enough, if he could get a weapon, maybe they could get out of this. Then he caught Winona giving him an intent look. Under her blanket a slight bulge appeared and was gone. It took him a few seconds to realize what she was trying to convey. He gave a barely perceptible nod and she silently mouthed the words, "I love you."

Winona firmed her hold on the pistol and said into Bright Rainbow's ear, "Now, child, now."

Bright Rainbow pushed off her and scampered to Nate's side and grabbed his arm.

Simultaneously, Winona cast off the blanket and lunged at Sacripant. Before he could blink she was next to him with the muzzle of her pistol pressed to his temple and her other hand on his throat. "If your friends try to harm us, you die."

BOOKS BY DAVID ROBBINS

Horror:
PRANK NIGHT
SPOOK NIGHT
HELL-O-WEEN
THE WERELING
THE WRATH
SPECTRE

Novels:
ANGEL U
HIT RADIO
BLOOD CULT
A GIRL,
THE END OF THE WORLD
AND EVERYTHING

Westerns:
BLOOD FEUD
THUNDER VALLEY
RIDE TO VALOR
DIABLO

Series:
ENDWORLD
WILDERNESS
WHITE APACHE
DAVY CROCKETT

Nonfiction:
HEAVY TRAFFIC

WILDERNESS

#68

SAVAGE HEARTS

by

David Robbins

Published by Mad Hornet Publishing
Printed in the United States of America
ISBN 978-0-9839882-8-1

www.davidrobbinsauthor.com

MAD HORNET
PUBLISHING

Dedicated to Judy, Joshua and Shane.

CHAPTER ONE

They came out of the southwest, nine hard men on gaunt mounts. They looked back often but the dust cloud that had been a fixture in their lives for over three weeks was gone. Still, they pushed on.

They were caked with dust; their clothes, their saddles, their horses. Those without bandanas breathed dust, too. Not that they would complain. To complain would anger their leader and there was't a man among them who would dare his wrath.

El Gato, they called him. The Cat. He wasn't like a cat in any respect save one. He was big and heavy and bearded and had a belly that hung over his belt. His teeth were big, like a bull's, and his temper was a lot like a bull's, as well. For all his size, though, he was ungodly quick with his hands. He was so quick that few could draw and shoot as fast as he could, and no one was as quick with a knife. So they called him El Gato.

It was near evening on the twenty-third day of their flight that El Gato drew rein and looked back for the dust cloud that was no longer there. He grunted and announced, "We have lost them."

"More likely they gave up," Morton Thrack said. For an Americano his Spanish was excellent. He wore a wide-brimmed black hat and a black vest and had not one, not two, not even three but four flintlocks wedged under his belt. Next to El Gato, he had the quickest hands. Including El Gato, he was the most vicious, and the most feared.

"What I would like to know," said Pepe, pushing his sombrero back on his head, "is where in the hell we are?"

"We must be in Canada by now," Alvarez joked. "But I don't see any snow or moose."

"What are moose?" Sabino asked.

"It is like a deer only ten times as big," Alvarez said, "and has antlers as wide as your *madre's* ass. Out to there." He spread his arms their full length.

Several of the men laughed but Sabino scowled. "Always you make fun of me. I do not like you saying things about my mother."

"*Excusa*," Alvarez said. "Did I say your *madre*? I meant your *hermana*."

Sabino colored and placed his hand on his *pistola*. "You will apologize."

"Or what?" Alvarez said. "You will scare me with your looks?"

Their argument might have escalated had El Gato not twisted in his saddle and growled, "How about me, Alvarez? Do I scare you?"

"*Si*, El Gato," Alvarez said, and his tone made plain it was true.

"I do not want to hear another word about Sabino's mother or sister or brothers or dog or cat or goat or his feet or you will answer to me."

"What is wrong with my feet?" Sabino asked.

Alvarez said, "I meant no disrespect, El Gato."

"Is that so?" El Gato wheeled his horse. "Are you stupid, then?"

"I must be," Alvarez said.

"You always know just what to say," El Gato complimented him, "and you follow orders as good as any of the others. But you think you are a great jester and you say things you shouldn't and cause trouble for me."

"May I cut off my tongue if I ever do that."

"The next time you do, that is exactly what you will lose." El Gato reined back around and gazed out across the imposing array of miles-high peaks that stretched for as far as the eye could see. "The hell of it is, we could well be in Canada for all we know."

"Not anywhere close," Morton Thrack said. "If I had to guess, I'd say the middle of the Rockies. North of Pike's Peak and south of Long's Peak and to the west of both."

"That is some guess," El Gato said.

"I'm from up this way, remember?" Thrack leaned on his saddle horn. "It's funny. I went south because the law was after me and now I'm heading north because *soldados* are after us."

"They were." El Gato idly scratched his beard, and chuckled. "All because I make my living robbing and killing."

"Makes two of us. But some folks would say that's not really making a living."

"The day I care about what other people think is the day you can shoot me."

They pushed on. By late in the day they were miles farther and a mile higher. Spruce and firs and aspens replaced the cottonwoods and oaks. Marmots whistled, eagles screeched, and the deer showed no fear.

"Why don't they run off?" El Gato wondered.

"They've never seen anything like us before," Thrack said. "They don't know that we hunt them and eat them?"

"Can such a thing be?" El Gato marveled.

"Chipmunks will eat out of your hand and ravens will roost in the branches over your head."

"You exaggerate, my friend."

"There's no law, either."

El Gato drew rein so abruptly that the man behind him nearly rode into his horse. "No law? How is that possible?"

"It's not like Mexico where federal soldiers are everywhere," Thrack explained. "Far as I know, the nearest fort is Fort Leavenworth, six or seven hundred miles away."

"What about gringo lawmen?" El Gato asked. "The marshals. And what do you call them, the sheriffs?"

"There aren't any."

"Do you think I am dumb? Every gringo town has someone who wears a badge."

"That's just it," Thrack said. "There aren't any towns. The government bought all this land from the French, hell, thirty years ago. But they haven't done anything with it. There are a few trading posts like Bent's Fort and some settlers here and there but that's it. The rest is wilderness."

A gleam came into El Gato's dark eyes. "I want to be sure I understand. Are you telling me, *amigo*, that we can do all the things we did south of the border and no one will come after us to arrest us or execute us?"

"Unless things have changed since I've been away, there's no law at all."

"*Madre de Dios,*" El Gato said, and laughed. "Can this be? I have found heaven."

"You're not listening," Thrack said. "Most of it is wilderness. There aren't that many people to rob and kill."

"But there are some, *sí?*"

"*Sí.*"

"Then let us find a few and celebrate our good fortune by robbing and killing them." And with that El Gato whooped and spurred his horse.

CHAPTER TWO

Fester Simmons had been in the Rockies since the heyday of the free trappers. He'd stayed on after the beaver market hit bottom and most of the trappers still alive scattered to the four winds. He liked the mountains too much to leave. He had a cabin in the Sangre de Cristos and once a year he made a pilgrimage, as he liked to think of it, to Bent's Fort to sell the peltries he'd collected since his last visit and buy the few supplies he needed.

Fester would never admit it but he also liked to mingle with the traders and freighters and settlers. He could do without civilization, thank you very much, and he could do without people, but he did like to hear about what was going on in the rest of the world if only so he could laugh at his fellow man's follies.

It was that time of year again.

Fester came down out of the high country leading Marabell by the reins. For once she wasn't acting contrary, which made him suspect she was up to something. She was as independent and stubborn as a mule could be, and then some.

Now, walking along with the reins in one hand and his Hawken rifle in the crook of his elbow, Fester spat tobacco juice and wiped his mouth with the sleeve of his buckskins. "Yes, sir," he said. "I reckon as how I'll do it, by God. I've got me some prime plews and they should fetch enough that I can get me that knife I've been hankerin' after." He looked over his shoulder at Marabell who flicked her ears as if annoyed by his chatter.

"That's enough out of you, missy," he said.

Fester had long wanted a bowie. It was silly since he already owned a perfectly good hunting knife and three perfectly fine skinning knives, but he couldn't get the bowie he'd seen at the suttler's at Bent's last year out of his head. It wasn't just that it was the biggest knife he'd ever set eyes on. It was also the prettiest. The brass guard and pommel made it shine like the midday sun, and the blade gleamed like sterling silver.

"It's old age," Fester justified his love for the knife to Marabell. "We get weak in the head. If I was half the man I used to be, I'd keep my money in my poke."

They were winding up a game trail Fester always used. He was ten days or more away from Bent's yet and by the time he got there he would be tuckered out. His body wasn't what it once was.

"Course, I thought awful highly of the man, himself. Jim Bowie was the real article. It wasn't enough Bowie invented the best fightin' knife there ever was. He also went and gave his life at the Alamo."

Marabell had heard all this before and didn't seem the least bit interested.

"Remember that sandbar fracas I told you about? He was stabbed clean through and shot, and yet he cut the heart strings of one feller and used his knife on a couple of others, besides. The doc didn't expect Bowie to live but he was tough, Jim was."

They came to the crest of a ridge and Fester stopped to catch his breath. He took off his beaver hat and ran his tobacco-stained sleeve over his brow. "Sure is hot, ain't it? Even this high up."

Below them spread a long valley hemmed by timber.

Fester wound on down and was about halfway to the valley floor when he spied coils of smoke.

"A campfire, by God," he said, and stopped.

He was worried it might be hostiles. The Utes and him were on good terms but the Arapahos would as soon lift his hair over that time he helped himself to several of their horses. Thinking of it made him mutter, "Those damned redskins sure can hold a grudge."

Fester watched the smoke a while. A white man's fire, he decided. Indians were too smart to make that much smoke and give themselves away. His natural inclination was to give them a wide berth. Then again, it bothered him, white men so close to his cabin. Granted, it was nigh on to thirty miles, but to his way of reckoning, that was the same as being camped on his doorstep.

Fester turned north. He stayed in the woodland and moved slow so he'd see them before they saw him. He'd gone a considerable piece when he heard voices. They were speaking Spanish. That didn't surprise him much. A lot of freighters were Mexicans but if these were freighters they'd lost their way and strayed from the trail to Santa Fe.

Then Fester saw them. He counted seven, all of them wearing those high-crowned hats Mexicans liked.

Fester didn't care for their looks. Their hard faces were the stamp of hard men. He doubted there was any among them who'd had a bath in ages. Not that he had any room to talk, given as how he only ever took a bath once a year and had to force himself to take that.

The biggest of the Mexicans was also the loudest. He had a way of laughing that grated on Fester's ears. Fester didn't like that the man scratched himself so much, either. Fester had lice but he didn't keep at them every minute of the day.

"No, sir," Fester said quietly to Marabell, and turned to go back the way they came.

"Where do you think you're goin', old-timer?"

Fester gave a start. Two men had come up behind him and were covering him with pistols. The one who had addressed him wore a black hat and a black vest and had an armory around his waist. The man held a flintlock inlaid with silver.

"What's the meanin' of this?" Fester demanded.

The man in the black hat came up to Marabell and ran his free hand over Fester's peltries. "Not bad. Where are you goin' with these?"

"Bent's," Fester said. "Not that it's any of your business."

"How about you hand me that rifle."

"How about I don't."

The man in the black hat pointed his fancy pistol at Fester's face and thumbed back the hammer.

Fester was furious. He was also a little scared. It had been his experience that folks didn't go around pointing pistols unless they were up to no good. "I don't like this," he said. "I don't like it even a little bit." He held out his Hawken.

"Smart," the man in the black hat said. He gave the

rifle to the Mexican and took hold of Marabell's reins but when he tugged she didn't move. He tugged again and she flicked her ears and ignored him. "What's wrong with this critter?"

"She only goes for me."

The man shoved the reins at him. "Then make her go or we'll shoot her and tote the hides."

"You're not all that nice, mister," Fester said angrily.

"No," the man in the black hat said. "I'm not."

CHAPTER THREE

It was toward sunset when Winona King came out of the cabin and walked to the lake with her head bowed and her hands clasped behind her back. She had a decision to make. It was a hard decision but it had to be done. If she didn't do it now she might never sever the tie.

Winona sighed. A full-blooded Shoshone, she was in her middle years. Her hair was a lustrous black. She wore a soft doeskin dress decorated with blue beads that she had fashioned with her own hands.

Winona had a grown son who was married and a daughter who had designs on a young warrior who lived across the lake. She also had a girl from another tribe staying with them, and it was the girl who caused her so much sadness.

The child had come to live with them after her parents were slain by a mountain lion. That was more than two moons ago, and a decision was long overdue. Should they take the girl back to her people or let her stay and rear her as their own?

The door opened and closed and a large shadow spread over her and out over the water. "Husband," Winona said without looking.

Nate King put his arm around his wife's waist. A big man, broad of shoulder, he wore buckskins and moccasins, beaded as hers were. An ammo pouch, a powder-horn and a possibles bag crisscrossed his chest. Under his belt on either side of the buckle were a pair of flintlocks. In a sheath on his right hip rested a bowie. Wedged under his belt on his left hip was a tomahawk. "Wife," he said, and kissed her on the cheek.

"What is she doing?"

"Evelyn is teaching her checkers."

"Then we have a while. Not that we need it."

"You've already made up you mind, I take it?"

"Yes, but I want to hear your opinion before I say anything."

Nate kicked a pebble and it rolled into the water. He stared at the geese and ducks, in particular a mallard with young swimming in her wake. "We can't keep her. It wouldn't be right."

Winona frowned.

"She's not ours. She's a Tukaduka," Nate said. Or, he reflected, a Sheepeater, as whites liked to call them, since they were so fond of mountain sheep. "Some say her people are related to yours and that may be true but she deserves to be with her own kind."

"And her own family," Winona said. "She must have relatives."

"The trick will be finding them."

Nate was well aware that the Sheepeaters were scattered all over the central Rockies. They didn't live in villages like the Shoshones and the Crows. Each family had its own valley or high country park where they eked out a living the best they were able given that they didn't have horses and still used the bow and arrow instead of guns. "It could take weeks."

"If not longer." Winona rested her cheek on his chest and idly toyed with a whang. "We are agreed, then?"

"As usual." Nate had learned by experience to trust his wife's judgment. He'd be the first to admit she was smarter than he was. That she spoke half a dozen tongues fluently while he had barely mastered two was eloquent proof.

"We must tell her."

They turned and walked arm-in-arm to the cabin. From within came laughter.

"She will take it hard," Winona predicted.

"Can't be helped."

Nate opened the door and Winona preceded him. He shut the door behind him and leaned on it and folded his arms.

Their daughter, Evelyn, and the Tukaduka girl, Bright Rainbow, were at the table, the wooden checker board Nate had carved between them. Evelyn was explaining how the pieces moved in the Shoshone tongue and Bright Rainbow listened intently.

Winona took an empty chair. She smiled at the pair and placed her forearms on the table.

"Do you want to play her, Ma?" Evelyn asked in English.

"No, thank you. Your father and I need to have words with Bright Rainbow."

"Oh." Evelyn frowned and sat back. "About what we talked about the other night?"

"Yes."

"I'll be sorry to see her go," Evelyn said. "It's nice having a sister of sorts. Do you want me to go to my room so you can talk to her in private?"

"That will not be necessary." Winona focused on the smaller girl and switched to Shoshone. "How are you, Bright Rainbow?"

"Happy," she answered in her simple way. She had dark hair and bright eyes and had regained much of the weight she lost during her ordeal. "I like it here."

"We are glad," Winona said. "We have enjoyed having you. But it is time to think about returning you to your people."

Bright Rainbow was only twelve. She didn't have the artifice to hide her feelings, and her face mirrored her dismay. "I like it here," she repeated.

"And we like you," Winona said. "But we can't keep you forever."

"No, please," Bright Rainbow pleaded, her voice quavering.

Over at the door, Nate was puzzled by her reaction. He'd have thought she'd be tickled to return to her own kind. He caught Winona's eye and saw that she was as perplexed as he was.

"Why are you against the idea?" Winona asked.

"I like it here."

"You keep saying that," Winona said. "You liked it with your own family, too, didn't you?" She was making a point, nothing more.

"They are dead."

"And we are sorry for you," Winona said.

Bright Rainbow stared at the table. "My mother is dead. My father is dead. My brothers are dead."

"We are sorry," Winona said again.

"My family is no more." Bright Rainbow looked up

and managed a smile. "Your family is a good family. I want to be part of yours."

"Oh, Bright Rainbow."

"What is wrong? Why do you not want me?"

"It is not that." Winona glanced at Nate for support and he came to her aid.

"We do not have the right to keep you, little one. You must have grandparents or an uncle or aunt who will take you in."

"There is no one."

Winona made the clucking sound she often did when her own children were little and misbehaved. "You should not lie. You must have family somewhere."

"Tell us where and we will take you to them," Nate said.

Bright Rainbow looked at him and then at Winona. Suddenly she burst into tears, pushed back her chair and bolted for the door. Nate got out of her way and she threw the door open and ran out, crying.

Winona couldn't believe he had done that. Rising, she said, "Why did you let her go?"

"What was I supposed to do?" Nate replied. "Trip her and pin her to the floor?"

"Honestly. You men." Winona brushed by him and hurried out.

The girl was past the chicken coop and flying toward the woods.

"Bright Rainbow! Wait, please!"

Nate came out and stated the obvious, "She's not listening."

"Stay here. I'll go talk to her." Winona started off but stopped when he said her name.

Nate reached inside and produced her rifle from where she had leaned it against the wall. "Aren't you forgetting something?"

It was a cardinal family rule that they never went anywhere without their rifles. Pistols weren't enough. They didn't always stop the bigger meat-eaters and other menaces.

Nate tossed the Hawken and Winona caught it and turned and broke into a jog.

"Bright Rainbow! Wait."

Winona crossed to the forest and shadows closed around her. She expected to hear the girl crying or crashing through the brush but all was silent. "Bright Rainbow? Where are you?" When there was no reply she ventured deeper in. "Bright Rainbow?"

Winona saw no sign of her. She was beginning to think the girl had gone off to hide when she came to a clearing and there was Bright Rainbow, as rigid as a tree. With good reason.

Across the clearing stood a buffalo.

CHAPTER FOUR

Fester Simmons was mad as hell. They'd taken his rifle and pistol and his knife and now they'd undone the rope to his packs and the bearded bundle of lard they called their leader was fingering a bobcat plew.

"This is good fur, gringo. Very good," El Gato complimented his skill. "It will bring top dollar, si?"

"Better not get any dirt on it, damn you."

El Gato stopped fingering and glanced at Thrack. "Teach him some manners."

The back of Fester's head exploded in pain. He pitched to his hands and knees and thought for a few seconds that he would pass out.

El Gato was seated on a log that had been pulled close to the fire. Shifting, he slid his big boot under Fester's chin and tapped Fester's jaw. "I would be very careful what I say, were I you."

Fester wanted to jump up and slug him. But any sudden move on his part and he'd be shot to ribbons. "You talk big when your men have pistols pointed at me. Give me my flintlock or my knife and we'll go at it man to man."

"Listen to you," El Gato said, and laughed.

"How about I finish him?" Morton Thrack said.

"No," El Gato replied. "He amuses me, this one. The scrawny goat thinks he is a ram."

Fester rose to his knees and rubbed a knot on the

back of his head. Picking up his beaver hat, he jammed it on, and winced. "I know what all of you are, you gob of spit."

"What are we, old goat?"

"Robbers," Fester spat. "You aim to steal my plews and sell them for yourself but it won't work."

"And why not, may I ask?" El Gato said with mock civility.

"Because everybody in these parts knows my handiwork," Fester said. "The nearest place you can unload them is Bent's Fort, and St. Vrain and the Bent brothers will catch on right away whose they are."

"He's brag and bluff," Thrack remarked.

"Maybe not," El Gato said thoughtfully. He fingered the bobcat hide some more. "I have never felt fur so soft."

"There are other places besides Bent's," Thrack brought up.

Now it was Fester who laughed. "What are you goin' to do? Tote 'em all the way to St. Louis?"

"He mocks us," Alvarez said. "Let me slit his throat and be done with him."

"*Idiota*," El Gato said. "If I did not want Thrack to kill him, why would I want you to?"

"What use is he to us alive?" Alvarez asked. "He insults us and acts as if he is better than us, as all gringos do." He turned to Thrack. "Except you, of course."

"Maybe I will keep him as a pet," El Gato said, and a smirk split his wide face. He snapped his fingers at Pedro and said in Spanish, "A rope, quick." When Pedro brought one, El Gato drew his knife and cut off a six-foot length and made a loop at one end with a sliding knot. Chuckling, he held it out to Sabino. "Put this around the old goat's neck."

Fester hadn't been paying much attention to their yammering. He didn't speak their lingo and never cared to. It was enough that he spoke a few Injun tongues fairly tolerable. So he was taken aback when one of them came over and deftly flipped a rope around his neck. He grabbed the noose to tear it off and a pistol was shoved in his face.

"No, *senor*," Sabino said.

Fester glared at their big-bellied leader, who grinned fiendishly. "This is your doin', isn't it?"

"*Si*," El Gato said. "It is your—-." He stopped and glanced at Thrack and asked in Spanish, "What is the word? *Trailla?*"

"Leash," Thrack said.

El Gato laughed at Fester. "I have changed my mind about you. You are no longer a goat. You are a chicken."

"What?" Fester said.

"My uncle had a small farm, and he used to keep a chicken on a leash. Everyone thought he was *loco* but it was great fun to watch him walk his chicken." El Gato grinned. "From now on you are my chicken."

"Like hell I am, you crazy bastard." Fester gripped the rope with both hands.

"So long as you wear it, you live," El Gato said.

Fester hesitated.

"Go ahead," El Gato taunted. "Let me see how brave you are. Shows us you have *cojones*. Take the leash off and be shot. What are you waiting for? Or is it that you truly are a chicken?"

Fester unleashed a burst of profanity but all it did

was make El Gato laugh more.

"You see?" El Gato said to his men. "The old gringo loves us."

Alvarez shook his head. "There are times when I think you are *loco*."

"Do you even know how to think?" El Gato said.

"I think as good as anyone here."

"Is that so? Then why is it you always says things you shouldn't?"

Alvarez colored and was silent.

"See?" El Gato switched to English and addressed Fester. "You are not the only one who does not have *cojones*."

"I don't even know what that is," Fester said.

"It is these." El Gato cupped himself. "Me, I have huge ones. But you, you are a chicken." Cackling, he took the other end of the of the rope from Sabino and tugged. "On your feet, chicken."

Practically beside himself with fury, Fester stood. He yearned to punch his tormentor in the face but he wasn't anxious to be filled with lead. "I'll get you for this if it's the last thing I do."

"Spare me your threats, gringo." El Gato began a slow stroll around the fire, pulling Fester after him. "You see?" he said to the others. "Soon all of you will want a chicken like mine."

"*Loco*," Alvarez said.

Morton Thrack's mouth curled in a rare grin. "We should all be so crazy."

His circuit completed, El Gato pointed at the ground and said, "Sit, chicken."

"God, I hate you," Fester said, but he sat.

"You do not know when you are well off," El Gato told him. "Keep amusing me, my little chicken."

"And when I don't anymore?"

"When that happens," El Gato said ominously, "we pluck you and eat you."

CHAPTER FIVE

The Rockies were home to a shaggier cousin of the plains buffalo. Far fewer in numbers, they roamed in small herds. Reclusive, they avoided humans and were usually quick to melt away into the undergrowth. Usually. But now and then they were prone to charge, and the buff across the clearing gave every sign of doing just that. It pawed the ground and snorted and shook its huge head.

Bright Rainbow was rigid with fear.

Winona froze, too. Any movement, however slight, and the bull might attack.

She had her Hawken but she was reluctant to use it. Buffalo were incredibly hard to kill. Their skulls were so thick, the lead wouldn't penetrate. And a heart or lung shot didn't always bring them down, either. Their vitals were protected by thick layers of muscle and fat.

"Stay where you are," Winona whispered.

Bright Rainbow didn't respond.

Winona looked for other buffalo but didn't see any. She started to slowly sidle to the right for a better shot in case it rushed them, and nearly jumped when a hand fell on her shoulder.

"You shouldn't move, either," Nate whispered. He'd followed her because he felt they should talk to Bright Rainbow together. He didn't want the child to think that taking her back to her people was entirely Winona's idea, and think less of her.

Winona felt a wave of relief. Her man was a skilled shot and had killed his share of the brutes. With him there they stood a better chance.

Suddenly the bull sent a clod of dirt flying. It swung its head from side to side, its curved horns glinting like black scythes.

Bright Rainbow began to quake.

"Be still," Winona whispered.

Nate realized the bull was about to attack. The girl wouldn't stand a prayer. It would shatter half the bones in her body and pulp her flesh. A desperate gambit was called for.

Moving forward so the buffalo saw him, Nate raised his arms and shouted at the top of his lungs, "Ho! Get out of here, you mangy monster!"

Winona was dumfounded. She raised her rifle, ready to protect Nate.

For a few seconds the outcome hung on the cusp of uncertainty. The buffalo stopped snorting and stared at Nate in what might be bewilderment. Then, with a rumbling grunt, it wheeled and crashed off through the vegetation like a hairy battering ram.

"Thank God," Nate breathed.

Winona dashed to Bright Rainbow and enfolded the girl in her arms. "You are safe."

Bursting into tears, Bright Rainbow pressed her face to Winona's bosom.

"It's all right," Winona said. "Let it out."

Bright Rainbow cried a good long while. Finally she stepped back and bowed her head.

"You were very brave," Winona complimented her.

"You do not want me."

Winona realized she hadn't been crying because of the buffalo. "It is not a matter of wanting," she explained. "It is a matter of doing what is right. And it is right for you to be with your own people."

"Even when I want to be with you?"

"We must at least let them know you are alive," Winona said. "They might like a say in what is done with you."

"What if I ask them to let me stay? If they say yes would you have me?"

Winona was torn. She didn't want to raise another child. She didn't want to say no, either. Her husband spared her from having to respond by answering first.

"One step at a time, girl. First we find your people and talk it over with them. We'll head out in the morning."

"As you wish," Bright Rainbow said sorrowfully.

They headed back.

When they were almost to the front door, Nate stopped and said that he'd be back in a while. Going around the cabin, he went along the shore to another.

Of the four that ringed the lake, this cabin was unique. It was the only one with a steeple. Smoke curled from the chimney and Nate caught the scent of venison. Cradling his Hawken, he knocked. When no one came he knocked again.

"A pox on impatient people," boomed a voice inside. "Hold your horses. I'll be right there."

Nate gazed at a V of geese winging in over the lake and saw a bass jump.

The door was jerked open, framing a white-haired man in buckskins, his face as craggy as the mountains. In his right hand was a large wooden spoon, in his left a measuring cup. Around his waist was an apron spattered with flour.

"Oh my," Nate said. "Mrs. McNair, I presume?"

Shakespeare McNair blistered the air with oaths, ending with, "I should bean you with this spoon, Horatio. I'll have you know I'm fixing supper for my beloved."

"Where is she?" Nate asked on noticing that McNair was the only one there.

"She went to visit your oldest and his wife," Shakespeare said, moving to the counter.

Nate closed the door and took a seat at their table. "I don't believe I've ever seen you cook before."

"I do it all the time, I'll have you know."

"You should wear an apron more often. They become you."

"If my hands weren't full I'd shoot you." McNair pointed the spoon at Nate. "Thou art the best o' the cutthroats," he quoted his namesake.

Nate chuckled. His mentor owned a dog-eared copy of the Bard that he'd been reading for the better part of thirty years and could quote with amazing facility. "What have you done this time?"

"I beg your paltry pardon?"

"I know you. You wouldn't be standing there covered with flour without a reason. I suspect you're in hot water with Blue Water Woman and you're cooking supper to try and win her over."

"You have a great imagination proper to madmen,"

Shakespeare paraphrased as he got down the sugar from a cupboard.

"Look me in the face and tell me I'm wrong."

"I can't. I'm making a pie."

"I thought so."

"I scorn you, scurvy companion. Go pester the Blackfeet. They know how to deal with know-it-all upstarts." Shakespeare bent over a pie pan.

"What did you squabble about?"

"It wasn't a squabble so much as a tempest," Shakespeare informed him. "I happened to mention that I thought it silly of her to rebuff my advances when all she had was a cold."

"Why, you horn toad, you."

"I believe her exact words were 'randy rooster'," Shakespeare said.

"At your age. I'm shocked."

"At my age you should be impressed." Shakespeare picked up an apple he had already peeled and commenced to carve it into pieces, moving the blade with his thumb. "There are days when I think she indulges me just so I won't be grumpy."

"You? A grump? The mind boggles."

"In civility thou seem'st so empty," Shakespeare let fly with another barb.

"And here you've been complaining of late of aches and creaking joints," Nate reminded him. "It's nice to know that something works."

"A lip of much contempt speeds from me," Shakespeare quoted again, and resumed slicing. "To what do I owe this visit, anyway?"

"The Tukaduka."

"What about them?"

"They're scattered all over creation. I figured you might know of a family somewhere."

"I can go you one better," Shakespeare said. "At this time of year they come down out of the high country and get together for a spell."

This was news to Nate, and he said so.

"Find their camp and you'll have more Tukaduka than you know what to do with. They don't miss their great hunt."

Nate knew that the Shoshones and Crows and other mountain tribes made regular forays to the prairie to hunt buffalo. But he couldn't see the Tukaduka doing that, not when they didn't own horses. "What do they go after? Elk? Deer? Bear, maybe?"

Shakespeare looked at him and grinned and shook his head. "Grasshoppers."

CHAPTER SIX

They got underway late. Nate wanted to leave shortly after sunrise but Shakespeare and Blue Water Woman came to see them off and so did his son, Zach, and Louisa, Zach's wife, and everyone stood around talking until finally he climbed on his bay and announced, "We're heading out, dear." He added, so Winona wouldn't accuse him of being bossy, "If you don't mind, that is."

Shakespeare came over and gripped Nate's hand. "Keep your eyes skinned, Horatio. You're heading into some rough country."

"I should find the Tukaduka without much problem, thanks to you."

"Don't fret about Evelyn. The missus and me will help Zach and Lou look after her."

Winona reined her mare around. "I am ready when you are, husband."

Everyone smiled and waved except for Bright Rainbow. She rode with her head down and her lower lip quivering.

Nate half thought she would cry some more but to his relief she held it in.

At one time there was a pass over the divide to the west but Nate and Shakespeare had brought the rock walls crashing down with a keg of black powder when hostiles invaded King Valley. So now, Nate and Winona headed north to another pass only the family and their friends knew about.

The mountains were in the full bloom of summer, and bursting with life and vitality. Deer and elk grazed in the meadows. Marmots whistled and badgers surveyed the world from atop their dens. Squirrels and chipmunks were everywhere. Long-eared rabbits bounded off in prodigious leaps. Once, they glimpsed a grey fox.

Finches and grosbeaks and sparrows flitted amid the trees. Jays screeched and woodpeckers drilled rat-a-tat-tat. Ravens flapped on black-as-night wings, and high in the sky hawks and eagles soared.

Nate breathed deep of the mountain air, and was in heaven. He loved the Rockies. He'd never intended to make them his home when he first came west. But they got into his blood---nay, into his soul---and now he could no more leave the mountains than he could stop breathing.

It was a grand day with a bright sun and a sky as blue as anything.

They were through the pass by noon and by late afternoon were well along on their westward swing.

Nate had calculated that it would take them the better part of a week to reach the general area where Shakespeare believed the Tukaduka would be. He wasn't in any hurry. It was rare these days for him to get away with Winona, and he looked forward to their time together.

Nate was daydreaming about how enjoyable their return ride would be, with just the two of them, when the love of his life said his name. He glanced up, saw she was staring intently to the northwest, and looked in the same direction. He promptly drew rein.

Riders were crossing a ridge half a mile away. Five, Nate counted, and even at that distance he could tell they were Indians.

"Enemies, you think?" Winona said in mild annoyance. She'd hoped their journey would go without incident.

"Can't say. Let's hunt cover," Nate cautioned, and veered into the trees. She followed suit. They went a short way and he stopped and looked back to find that Bright Rainbow was still out in the open, sitting her horse and gazing glumly at the ground.

"She didn't hear you," Winona said.

"She'll get us killed, she keeps this up." Nate cupped a hand to holler but thought better of the notion and rode back out.

Bright Rainbow didn't raise her head until he was next to her and touched her arm.

"Don't your ears work?"

She blinked in confusion.

Nate pointed at the distant riders.

Bright Rainbow blanched. "I am sorry. I am lost in my sadness."

"We'll remedy that."

Bending, Nate snatched the reins from her hand and led her mount into the woods. She didn't object or try to wrest the reins free. Dismounting, he let his own reins dangle. "Keep an eye on her," he advised Winona, and hurried to where he could observe the riders without being seen.

The five riders had descended the ridge and were striking out across the valley. They rode in single file and each had a bow or a lance.

If Nate had to guess, he would say they were Utes or Nez Perce. He was on good terms with both so there was no reason to hide, but then again, he could be wrong. He sought telltale clues in their hair and their horses but he'd need the vision of a bird of prey to see them clearly that far off. In any event, the five were heading east and not west and posed no threat. He watched until they were out of sight and stayed put an extra couple of minutes to be sure.

"Is it safe?" Winona asked as he strolled back.

"Safe as can be," Nate answered with complete confidence. He handed Bright Rainbow's reins up and she gripped them with no enthusiasm. "But she's not helping things."

Winona kneed her mare alongside the girl's dun. "You must stop behaving like this."

"I told you," Bright Rainbow said. "I am sad."

"Keep on as you are and you could get us killed," Winona scolded.

"I would not want that."

"Then stay alert. For all our sakes."

Nate led them out of the trees and went to rein to the west. Too late, he spotted three more riders coming over the distant ridge. More of the same band, he reckoned, and tried to regain cover. But even as he hauled on his reins, one of them raised an arm in his direction and all of them stopped.

They had seen him.

CHAPTER SEVEN

Nate fled, Winona and Bright Rainbow close behind. He didn't know if the Indians were hostile but he couldn't take the chance.

They hadn't gone a hundred yards when Nate looked back and frowned. Bright Rainbow was trying her best but she had never been on a horse before she came to stay with them, and while Winona and Evelyn had given her lessons, and Bright Rainbow could handle a horse at a walk, at a gallop she flopped and jounced and clung to the dun's mane in stark fright. He drew rein again.

"What is wrong?" Winona asked.

Nate nodded at the girl. "She'll fall off and break her neck."

"Ah." Winona wheeled her mare and held out her arm. "Get on behind me."

Bright Rainbow didn't hesitate. She swung across and wrapped her arms around Winona's waist, clinging tight.

Nate snagged the dun's reins. "Ride like the wind," he said, and did so for almost a mile. Figuring that should be enough, he brought the lathered bay to a stop and twisted in the saddle.

"Any sign of them?" Winona anxiously asked.

"Not a hair."

Winona lowered Bright Rainbow and climbed down. She put her hand to the small of her back and arched it to relieve stiff muscles. It had been a while since she'd ridden so hard. "Wouldn't it be ironic if we went to all this trouble and they are friendly?"

"Better safe than sorry," Nate said.

Bright Rainbow looked at both of them in confusion. She didn't speak English but she must have divined they were talking about the warriors because she said in Shoshone, "They might be Bloods."

Nate doubted it. The Bloods were part of the dreaded Blackfoot Confederacy. The Kainai, they called themselves, and lived in southern Canada. "They hardly ever come this far south."

"They might be Bloods," Bright Rainbow said again.

"Why do you say that?" Winona asked.

"They are mad at my people."

Nate and Winona looked at one another, and Winona said, "Why are they mad?"

"They want their stick back."

"What in blazes is she talking about?" Nate said in English.

Winona squatted and placed her hand on the girl's shoulder. "We do not understand."

"My father took us to the great hunt every summer," Bright Rainbow informed them. "It was a happy time. We ate a lot and laughed a lot and I played with other children."

"The stick?" Winona prompted.

"One day two summers ago some warriors went to hunt deer. When they came back, they brought a hurt man they had found. He had an arrow in his side. He was a Blood. My people tried to help him but he died."

When she didn't go on, Winona said, "That still doesn't explain the stick."

"The Blood had it with him. He had a bow and a fine knife and other things. One was a long stick with feathers on it."

"A coup stick," Nate figured. A warrior struck an enemy with it to gain esteem among his people for courage.

"Your people kept the man's things?" Winona asked.

"Yes. Then after some moons had passed, we heard that Blood warriors were looking for the dead man and his stick."

That made no sense to Nate. Coup sticks were easy enough to replace when they were broken or lost.

Winona stood. "Whoever they are, we must not let them catch us. We should be on our way."

"We can take a couple of minutes more." Nate was thinking of their horses. He stared back the way they had come and felt his pulse quicken at the sight of riders weaving among tall firs half a mile back. "Consarn it all."

"This is not good, husband," Winona said.

Nate considered that an understatement. He bid her to mount, then swung Bright Rainbow on behind her. Once more he set out with the dun's reins in his hand.

Winona came up next to him. "How do you want to do this?" she loudly asked to be heard above the thud of hoofs.

"We stay ahead of them until dark and lose them once night falls."

When next Nate looked back he didn't see their

pursuers. For the next several hours they pushed on, stopping periodically to rest their horses. The sun was setting when he came to yet another halt and scanned their back trail. "So far, so good."

Winona slid off the mare and helped Bright Rainbow down. "If they are Bloods, they have not chased us because of any coup stick. They must know you are a white man."

Nate grunted. Thanks to Lewis and Clark, the Blackfoot Confederacy hated whites. Lewis and some of his men shot a Blackfoot and stabbed another when the warriors tried to take their guns. The depth of the Blackfoot hatred ran so deep that any whites they came across, they killed. It was said that they would chase a white man to the ends of the earth, if need be.

And now he might have eight of them after him.

CHAPTER EIGHT

Winona didn't let on how worried she was. She considered it a bad omen that they had run into probable enemies so early in their journey. Her husband liked to tease that she read too much into signs. She always countered that he didn't read enough.

Winona wished Zach was along. She'd never admit it to Nate, but while he was a good protector, their son was the fiercer warrior. She sometimes wondered if that was because Zach had her blood as well as Nate's. Until he was married, Zach had lived to count coup, as every Shoshone warrior did.

"Will those warriors catch us?" Bright Rainbow ended Winona's reverie.

"Not if we have a say," Winona answered, and ran her hand over the girl's head.

"My people are afraid of them."

"They should be," Winona said. The Tukaduka weren't fighters. Some tribes didn't even consider them warriors. The Sheepeaters didn't count coup and never went on the war path. They were content to live in peace with everyone and devoted themselves to their families and their people.

More than once over the years, Winona had thought how wonderful it would be if more tribes were like them.

Bright Rainbow had more on her mind. "Why is there so much to be afraid of all the time?"

"It is life," Winona said. "It is how things are and how they have always been and perhaps how they will always be."

"I do not like being scared."

"No one does, little one."

Nate was pacing with one eye on the sky. Stars had blossomed like so many celestial fireflies. "It's almost time."

Winona brought Bright Rainbow over to the horses. "Do you intend to push on until dawn?" she asked in English.

"It would be best."

"I'm thinking of her," Winona said, with a nod at their charge.

"Let me know when we have to stop, then."

Well off in the timber a wolf howled. To the east a coyote yipped. The nocturnal feast of the meat-eaters was underway. From dusk until daybreak, the deadly dance of predator and prey stained the earth red with blood.

Nate held to a careful walk. To go faster invited calamity. There were too many hazards; too many logs, too many boulders, too many deadfalls.

With the pale starlight to illuminate their way and a cool breeze on their faces, they covered mile after mile.

Winona made sure that Bright Rainbow kept her arms around her waist and told her that if she started to doze off, she should say something. The girl promised she would. But along about midnight Winona felt her arms slacken and then the feel of Bright

Rainbow's forehead on her back. She glanced over her shoulder and said softly, "Bright Rainbow?"

Bright Rainbow snapped her head up. "Sorry," she said.

"Do we need to stop?"

"No. It will not happen again."

But half an hour later, it did. Bright Rainbow's body sagged and her arms went limp, and Winona drew rein. "Husband," she said.

Nate had hoped to get farther. While Winona spread their blankets, he stripped the horses and hobbled them so they wouldn't stray. He didn't kindle a fire. It might be seen.

His back to a pine, Nate eased down and placed his Hawken across his legs.

Winona had placed Bright Rainbow on the blankets and now she curled onto her side and looked at him. "Can you go without a hug tonight?"

Nate grinned. "I'll try."

He sat listening to the roars and howls and shrieks until the wee hours. Eventually his chin dipped and he slept soundly until the chirp of a black-capped chickadee woke him.

A pink hue to the east heralded the new day.

Nate yawned and stretched and stiffly rose. He checked that the horses were still there, and turned. His wife was on her back, beautiful in repose, Bright Rainbow's cheek on her shoulder. He let them sleep a little longer while he walked in a wide circle. Save for the stirring of the songbirds, the forest was still.

Nate deemed it safe to start a small fire. He gathered broken pieces of downed branches and grass for kindling. Using his fire steel and flint, he sparked tiny flames and puffed them to life. He filled the coffee pot with water from the water skin and put it on to brew, then took a bundle of pemmican from a parfleche and unwrapped the hide. Dragging a log over to sit on, he was munching pemmican and waiting for the coffee to get hot when the love of his life stirred and smacked her lips and opened her eyes.

"Breakfast is about to be served, madam. I trust the gracious lady slept well?"

Winona grinned. One of the things that attracted her to him back when they first met was his playful streak. "You almost sound like Shakespeare."

"I hope not. My mind must be going."

Winona laughed. "If he heard you say that, he would blister your ears with the Bard."

Nate chuckled. "Once he called me the Mars of Malcontents, whatever that means. Another time I was a crusty botch of nature."

"How does he remember all that?"

Nate bit off a piece of pemmican and with his mouth full said, "You're a fine one to talk."

"What do you mean?"

"You speak how many tongues? Six? Seven? You even speak my own better than I do. And McNair has about memorized every page in that book of his, which is thicker than my arm." Nate shook his head in self-deprecation. "Compared to the two of you, I'm a dunce."

"Hardly that, husband," Winona said fondly. "You have a keen mind. And you read a lot. Show me another person within a thousand miles who owns as many books as you do."

"Fat lot of good all that reading has done me," Nate said. "I can't quote much of it."

"Reading is something you enjoy, as I enjoy sewing and knitting."

"I'm just not very smart," Nate said.

Behind him, a voice with a thick accent said, "No, *mon ami*, you are not."

Nate clawed for a pistol and leaped to his feet, and froze. He was the center of a ring of rifles and bows with arrows knocked to sinew strings.

CHAPTER NINE

Fester Simmons would be damned if he'd be anybody's chicken. It was his opinion that the bandit called El Gato was crazier than a loon, and the sooner they parted company, the healthier he'd stay. The others were vermin. Murderous vermin, so he had to be careful how he went about it.

Fester had decided the best time to sneak away was right before dawn. Usually only one man was on guard and half asleep by the fire.

The problem was, before turning in they always tied his wrists and ankles. But seeing as how they weren't too bright and tied his hands in front of him, once they were snoring he commenced rubbing the rope against a jagged rock he'd palmed when no one was looking.

It took hours. Fester's arms and shoulders were welters of pain when the rope finally parted. He rubbed his wrists to relieve the pain while watching the man at the fire from under hooded lids. Then he set to work on his ankles.

Alvarez was the sentry. He sat on a log facing the fire with his rifle across his legs.

Dumb as a rock, Fester thought, and almost cackled out loud. Anyone with half a brain knew you didn't stare directly into a fire. Not when hostiles or a bear might jump you. It blinded you when you looked into the dark, long enough for a hostile to slit your throat or for a bear to separate your head from the rest of you.

Alvarez's chin bobbed. It would dip and he'd jerk it up and shake himself and then after a while it would dip again.

By the stars Fester reckoned it was past three. That gave him about an hour and a half, maybe a bit longer. He pred and pried and finally the knots gave way.

Alvarez still hadn't fallen asleep.

Fester waited some more and finally decided he'd waited long enough. If Alvarez didn't have the courtesy to doze off, he'd help things along. He cast about for a sizeable rock or a hefty chunk of wood but none was handy.

A rifle would make a dandy club but the bandits slept with them. He was debating whether to try for one when the nearest bandit rolled onto his back.

A pistol butt stuck from under the man's belt.

Fester licked his lips as if the pistol were a juicy steak. Keeping one eye on Alvarez, he slid toward the sleeper. A twig crunched and he turned to stone but Alvarez didn't look his way. Emboldened, he reached over, lightly gripped the flintlock, and started to ease it free.

The sleeper opened his eyes.

"Well, hell," Fester said out loud, and yanking the pistol out, he whipped it over his head and smashed it down with all his might. Something crunched, and Fester was up and running. He heard a squawk from Alvarez. A rifle boomed but by then he was in the trees and the slug smacked a bole and not his body. He ran for a good quarter of an hour, all the while grinning with delight at the yells and curses vented by his pursuers.

At length the sounds faded.

Fester stopped and leaned against an oak. His hands on his knees, he sucked in deep breaths. He was about done in. That was the most he'd run in a coon's age. He snickered at how mad the bandits must be. "Yes, sir, that was slick."

Then he realized that they still had Marabell. They still had his plews, too. As if that weren't bad enough, they also had his rifle and his pistol and everything else.

"Damn."

Fester chided himself for not thinking his escape through more carefully. Now he had to go back.

When he could breathe normally again, Fester straightened and retraced his steps. It was still dark and the forest canopy hid most of the stars so he had to rely on his sense of direction. Fortunately, it seldom failed him.

Dawn was breaking when Fester spotted the bright orange of their fire. Soon he could smell it. Flattening, he crawled until he could see them. And got a surprise.

They were all up. El Gato was seated on the log, grinning at Alvarez. Alvarez had been tied to a tree, and from the look of his battered face, badly beaten. Blood trickled from a corner of his mouth and his nose.

El Gato said something in Spanish. Alvarez hissed words in return and tugged at the ropes binding him. El Gato laughed.

The way Fester figured it, El Gato was punishing Alvarez for letting him get away. Some of the others didn't look too happy about it but no one came to Alvarez's defense.

Mortan Thrack didn't seem to have any interest at all. He was sipping coffee from a tin cup and not even looking at Alvarez.

Fester crawled in a half circle until he saw Marabell. She was picketed with the horses. His bundle of plews was nearby.

Fester hefted the flintlock. He had one shot and must use it wisely. Snaking into tall grass, he inched closer.

El Gato was doing more talking. Whatever he said made some of the bandits laugh.

Alvarez struggled and swore.

El Gato got up. Smiling, he stepped to the fire and took hold of the coffee pot by the handle. Still smiling, he turned and walked up to Alvarez and dashed the scalding hot coffee in Alvarez's face.

Alvarez screamed.

Fester was glad for the ruckus. It kept the bandits occupied. He crawled to the horse string and tried to undo the picket rope but the knots were too tight. He pried with his fingernails and broke one.

Marabell was staring at him as if she was trying to figure out what he was doing.

Fester smiled affectionately and whispered, "I'll have you out of here in three shakes of a lamb's tail, girl."

"No," Morton Thrack said above him, "you won't."

Fester rolled over, and blinked. The tip of Thrack's pistol was inches away. "Damn it to hell. I'd of heard you come up on me if that sissy Mex wasn't blubberin' like a damn baby."

"No," Morton Thrack said, "you wouldn't."

"You're awful cocky."

"Speaking of which," Thrack said, and thumbed back the hammer. "Your choice, old man. I can blow your brains out or you can give up."

Fester stared into the gun barrel and then into the killer's ice-cold eyes, and coughed. "Bein' a sissy is contagious."

CHAPTER TEN

There were eight of them but only seven were warriors. Blood warriors, as Bright Rainbow had warned they might be and Nate had hoped they weren't.

The last man was a mix. He had Indian features but paler skin. Where the rest wore their hair long, either loose or in a braid, his was cropped just below the ears. He had a rifle and a pair of pistols but he didn't point them at Nate or Winona. Grinning, he said, "*Parlez-vous francais?*"

"What?"

"I will take that as *non.*" With a grand sweep of his arm, the man bowed. "Permit me to introduce myself. I am Sacripant. I am, as you Yankees would say, a *trappeur.* Or sometimes you call us *voyageurs.*"

"I've met some of your kind," Nate said. Back during his trapping days, and after.

"You have a name, too, *oui?*"

"Nate King."

Sacripant looked at Winona and then at Bright Rainbow. "Your woman and your *petite,* eh?"

"The girl's not ours—-," Nate began, and stopped.

"Your *joli* woman, she is what? I am no great judge but I would say she is Crow, perhaps? Or maybe she is Shoshone?"

"Shoshone," Nate confirmed.

"And the little one?"

Nate saw no reason to lie. "Tukaduka."

"Is that so? Interesting," Sacripant said. "We will talk about that some more. But first I must ask you to place your pistols and your big knife and your tomahawk on the ground." He held up a hand when Nate went to speak. "I am afraid if you do not, my friends will kill you where you sit. They are not as nice as me."

Nate gazed at each of the warriors and saw no hint of friendliness.

"I am waiting, *monsieur*."

Nate squared his shoulders. "I'd be a fool to disarm if you intend to hurt my wife and the girl."

"It would be foolish not to. You might get one or two of them, but really now," Sacripant said, and gestured at the ring of weapons. "In any event, we do not make war on women and children. You have my word they are perfectly safe for the moment."

The *voyageur* was right. Nate would drop some of them and then be riddled with arrows and slugs. Reluctantly, he slowly placed his armory on the grass.

"There. That wasn't so hard, was it?" Sacripant addressed the warriors in their tongue. Several lowered their weapons. Others didn't.

Sacripant smiled. "*Tres bon*. Now we can—-." He started to turn toward Winona and Bright Rainbow, and stiffened. "*Mon dieu!*"

Unnoticed under her blanket, Winona had drawn one of her two pistols and now she brought it out and trained it on the halfbreed. "Tell your friends to drop their weapons or I will shoot you."

Sacripant laughed.

"If you think I won't, you're mistaken."

"Oh, I believe you, madam," Sacripant said. "It is just that you would shoot me for nothing. They are my friends, yes, some of them. But they are also Kainai. They would never surrender to a woman."

"They don't care if I shoot you?" Winona said skeptically. A glance at the warriors disabused her of her disbelief. Their faces might as well be sculpted in stone.

"It is not that they would not care so much as they could not bear the shame," Sacripant said. "For myself, I am not eager to die. If you would be so good as to set your flintlock aside, I would be grateful."

"You have a glib tongue," Winona said.

"I am part French, *oui?* And the French are great talkers. They would rather talk than do most anything except eat and *faire l'amour.*"

"And what?"

"Make love, my dear," Sacripant said. "I have often thought that if wars were fought by making love, the French would conquer the world."

"Enough," Nate said.

"My apologies, *monsieur*," Sacripant said with another of his bows. "I forget my manners sometimes." He grinned at Winona. "The *pistolet*, if you do not mind."

Winona glanced at Nate and Nate nodded. She set the flintlock on the ground and it was snatched up by a Blood warrior.

"*Merci*," Sacripant said. "Now then, suppose we sit

around your fire and have a little talk."

Nate fumed. But what choice did he have? He eased down next to Winona as she was sitting up with Bright Rainbow in her arms. "Sorry," he said.

"For what?"

"They took me by surprise."

"Don't be so hard on yourself." Winona felt Bright Rainbow shift and knew the girl was awake but shamming sleep. She didn't let on. The blanket fell around her waist and she left it there; it concealed her other pistol and her knife.

Sacripant sat cross-legged across from them and held his palms out to the fire. "Nate King," he said, his brow puckered. "Do you have a Shoshone name as well?"

"The Cheyenne gave me one a long time ago," Nate said. "Most tribes have called me by it ever since."

"Are you going to tell me or must I guess?"

Winona answered before Nate could. "My husband is known as Grizzly Killer," she said proudly.

"I thought as much," Sacripant said. "We have heard of this man of yours. He has counted coup on many of our brothers in the Blackfoot Confederacy, yes?"

"On a few," Nate acknowledged. "Only in self-defense."

"I am sure it was," Sacripant said, and laughed. He rubbed his hands together and looked at Bright Rainbow. "But now to business, as you whites say. My friends and I would like to ask a favor of you."

"What kind of favor?" Nate asked. "And what if I say no?"

"Should you refuse, *monsieur*," Sacripant said, suddenly somber, "it would be most unfortunate for you and your lovely wife."

CHAPTER ELEVEN

Fester couldn't take the screams after a while. It reminded him of the Apaches, the things El Gato did to Alvarez. He noticed that the rest of the bandits didn't laugh after El Gato pulled out his knife and set to work.

As for him, they'd bound his wrists and ankles again, tighter than the last time. He lay curled on his side with his back to the carving and wished he could plug his ears. The blubbering at the end was the worst. He didn't know much Spanish but he recognized begging when he heard it. There was a last gurgle and then a whine, and footsteps came up behind him and a foot struck him low in the back. He looked up.

"Did you hear, chicken?"

"How could I not?" Fester rejoined. He glanced at the tree and cursed. The image would be seared in his mind for as long as he lived.

El Gato was spattered with wet scarlet drops and his knife dripped crimson. Squatting, he wiped it back and forth on the grass to clean the blade. "I could tell you that was your fault, you know."

"Mine?"

"*Sí*. He let you escape. But I will be honest. He had been a---how do you gringos say it? A thorn in my side for a long time now, and I was tired of it. I had been looking for an excuse to kill him and you gave it to me. For that I thank you."

"Go to hell," Fester said.

"Why, little chicken? What is the matter? Are you squeamish?"

"No one deserves that."

El Gato cocked his head. "What does deserve have to do with it? Does anyone deserve to die?"

"You do."

El Gato chuckled. "I see. I am evil so I have no right to live. Fortunately for me, God does not think like you do."

Fester rose on an elbow. "Don't you dare. No one can do what you just did and claim to believe in the Almighty."

El Gato put a hand to his chest. "Why, little chicken, you have hurt my feelings," he said, and laughed. "Of course I believe in God." He gestured. "All you see around you was made by Him, was it not?"

"The Bible says it was. I can't read but my ma could and she read it every evening to us when we were younguns and then drug us to church every Sabbath. Next, I suppose you're goin' to say you believe in the Bible, too?"

El Gato slid his knife into a leather sheath on his hip. "What I believe, chicken, is that God and I are a lot alike."

"Now I've heard everything."

The bandit leader eased down and made himself comfortable. "I am in a good mood, so I will explain. My madre was a lot like yours. She had a Bible, too. And she dragged us to church and made us sit and listen to the priest and go to confession. She said it would help us grow to be good and decent. But do you know what?"

Fester waited.

"I have never liked good and decent, little chicken. Good and decent is boring. I was always doing things that got me in trouble. For instance, when I was a boy, I would catch lizards and chop them into pieces to see how long it took them to die."

"You're sick inside," Fester said.

"You have never done that? Never killed for the fun of it?"

Fester recollected his boyhood and a few birds he'd beaned with rocks and frogs he'd bashed and the time he set some ants on fire, and he didn't answer.

"Ah. Then you have? And are you sick inside, too?"

"Bashin' a frog ain't the same as *that*," Fester said, and bobbed his head at the tree.

"Where is the difference?"

"If I have to explain, you'd never savvy."

"No, chicken, it is you who do not understand. God kills all the time. He makes all of this, all the life, all the people and the animals, and what happens to them? They all die. God is the biggest killer there is."

Fester was flabbergasted. "That's the stupidest notion I ever heard."

"Where is it stupid, my little chicken? Each day how many people die in this world? Thousands, I should think. How many of them are stabbed and shot or burned to death or eaten by animals or die of sickness?" Now it was El Gato who shook his head. "No, I am right. God kills. And if I kill, too, then I am just like

Him. And if I am evil, then God is, too."

"You're twistin' my head into knots," Fester said. He knew the bandit was wrong but for the life of him he couldn't think of how to prove it.

"If anything, chicken, I am more honest than most. I admit how God is. My mother and your mother and others hide from the truth. They do not want to admit it. Not that I blame them. It is easier to pretend God is love than to admit that we are born just to die."

"There's more to life than that," Fester insisted.

"Why, yes, chicken, there is. There are *putas* and whiskey and the pleasure I will feel when I tire of you and do to you as I did to Alvarez. It gives you something to look forward to, no?"

And El Gato beamed.

CHAPTER TWELVE

Nate King kept hoping the Bloods would relax their vigilance. It was a futile hope. Three or four held weapons on him at any given moment. When he went to scratch an itch and raised his hand too quickly, rifles were jerked to shoulders and bow strings were pulled back.

"I would be careful, were I you, Grizzly Killer," Sacripant cautioned. "A man of your reputation, it makes my friends nervous."

"I do?" Nate said.

"Another sudden move like that, and do not blame me if you are made to look like a porcupine."

"You said something about a favor," Winona reminded him. That the Bloods hadn't slaughtered them outright gave her cause for optimism. But at the same time she didn't trust their halfbreed ally. Not because he was a breed. Her husband was white, after all, and their children of mixed blood. No, she didn't trust Sacripant because of how he looked at her.

"*Oui, une faveur*," he said, propping his hands behind him. "First I must tell you why we are here. We are very far from Blood territory and you perhaps wonder why."

"It did cross my mind," Nate said.

"One of us," Sacripant said, and pointed at a grim-faced warrior holding a rifle, "seeks something that belonged to his father."

"A coup stick."

Sacripant's mouth fell open in surprise. He glanced at Bright Rainbow and said, "Ah. The girl has told you about it? Good."

"Why all this bother?" Nate asked. "A coup stick is easy to replace."

"That is true," Sacripant conceded. "But this is no ordinary stick."

"How so?"

Sacripant indicated the grim-faced warrior again. "He is known as *Niukskai-Stamik*. In your tongue, Three Bulls. His father, Spotted Wolf, was a great war chief of the Kainai."

"Was?" Nate said, thinking of the story Bright Rainbow told them.

"Two winters past Spotted Wolf led a war party into Nez Perce country. Twenty of our best fighters went with him. They came on a Nez Perce village with many horses."

The Nez Perce, as Nate well knew, bred some of the best mounts anywhere. He also knew that to the Blackfeet and their allies, stealing a horse was accounted as high a coup as killing an enemy.

"The raid did not go well," Sacripant went on. "A horse guard saw them and gave the alarm. The Nez Perce rushed from their lodges in great numbers, and Spotted Wolf was driven back. Two of our warriors died. Several more were wounded. Spotted Wolf took an arrow in the side. The war party scattered with the Nez Perce after them."

"Some must have made it back," Nate guessed. Otherwise, Sacripant wouldn't know all this.

"*Oui.* All but the two who died at the village, and Spotted Wolf." Sacripant motioned at Three Bulls. "His son wanted to find out what happened to him. He returned to Nez Perce country and took a Nez Perce warrior captive. The warrior was made to talk."

Nate could imagine how.

"Three Bulls learned that the Nez Perce chased his father for more than ten sleeps but never caught him. They did come on some Tukaduka who told them that they had found Spotted Wolf hurt and dying and tried to help him but he was too far gone."

The account, Nate reflected, tallied with Bright Rainbow's.

"Spotted Wolf died and the Tukaduka buried him. They kept his horse and his clothes and his bow and arrow and the coup stick. Three Bulls wants it back."

"Again, why go to so much trouble?" Nate asked.

"Spotted Wolf's father made the stick and gave it to Spotted Wolf when he became too old to go on the war path. Spotted Wolf intended to do the same and give it to Three Bulls one day."

"Ah," Nate said.

"Do you see now? Three Bulls loved his father very much. To have the stick is to have part of his father, always."

"Has he asked the Tukadukas to give it back?"

"We have tried. But they run off like rabbits at the mere sight of us."

"Who can blame them?" Nate said. "The Bloods aren't known for their friendly dispositions."

Sacripant sighed. "It would make it easy for everyone if your friends would hear us out and give us the coup stick. That is all we want. Three Bulls has no desire to hurt them. He only wants the stick."

"Our friends?" Nate said.

Sacripant pointed at Bright Rainbow. "You must be on good terms with them. Why else would you have a Tukaduka child with you?"

"Her parents were killed and she's been living with us," Winona said. "We are returning her to her people."

"All the better." Sacripant grinned and said something in the Blood tongue to Three Bulls, who nodded. "It is good we saw you and were curious and came to see who you are. You can do what we can not."

"How do you mean?" Nate asked.

"That favor I talked about. Although now I see a swap is better."

"Swap what?" Winona said.

"Why, the girl for the coup stick, of course. Then will come the second swap."

"Second?" Nate said, confused.

Sacripant grinned. "You will bring the stick to us and swap it for your wife."

"What?"

"She stays with my friends and I until you bring us the coup stick. Do not fear. She will not come to harm. You have my word."

Anger welled, and Nate almost sprang at Sacripant then and there. "There's no need for you to hold her hostage. Let her come with me. I promise I'll bring the coup stick back."

"With my way you have more incentive."

"Damn you," Nate growled.

"Now, now."

Winona was dismayed. "What if the Tukadauka won't give him the stick?"

Sacripant shrugged. "Then I am afraid, madam, that you will spend the rest of your days in a Blood lodge with a Blood husband. Whether you want to or not."

CHAPTER THIRTEEN

Winona was glad she had another pistol hidden under the blanket. Shifting, she moved Bright Rainbow from one shoulder to the other, and as she did, she slipped her hand under the blanket and palmed the flintlock. Into Bright Rainbow's ear she whispered, "When I say to move, I want you to slide off me."

Nate glared at Sacripant. "I'm not leaving my wife here with you."

"I am afraid you do not have a say in the matter."

"I don't mind helping Three Bulls get the coup stick but my wife goes with me," Nate insisted.

"You are not listening, *monsieur.* What you want is unimportant." Sacripant laughed. "I must translate for my friends. Sit there and behave." He turned toward Three Bulls and launched into the Blood tongue.

Careful that they wouldn't see her mouth moving, Winona whispered to Bright Rainbow. "These are bad men. We must get away from them. When I let go of you, move to my husband and take his hand."

Bright Rainbow cracked her eyes so only Winona could see. "I will do whatever you want."

Winona slowly thumbed back the hammer, glad the blanket muffled the click. The Bloods, she saw, were listening to Sacripant. Guns and arrows were still pointed at Nate but not at her. Apparently, since she was female, they didn't think she was dangerous. Their mistake.

Nate girded himself to move. If he could spring fast enough, if he could get a weapon, maybe they could get out of this. Then he caught Winona giving him a meaningful look. Under her blanket a slight bulge appeared and was gone. It took him a few seconds to realize what she was trying to convey. He gave a barely perceptible nod and she silently mouthed the words, "I love you."

Winona firmed her hold on the pistol and said into Bright Rainbow's ear, "Now, child."

Bright Rainbow pushed off her, scampered to Nate's side, and grabbed his arm.

Simultaneously, Winona cast off the blanket and lunged at Sacripant. Before he could blink, she was next to him with the muzzle of her pistol pressed to his temple and her other hand on his throat. "If your friends try to harm us, you die."

Sacripant stiffened. "Oh, madam," he said. "What do you think you are doing? I have already explained what they will do."

A Blood warrior trained his rifle on Winona and addressed her in their language.

"He says if you do not lower your pistol," Sacripant translated,"he will shoot you."

"Tell him to go ahead."

"You want him to shoot you?"

"He does, and you can forget your swap," Winona said. "And Three Bulls can forget his father's coup stick."

Sacripant considered that and said something that

convinced the warrior to lower his rifle and the others to do the same with their weapons. "You have conquered us, *belle jeune fille*," he said with a grin. "What now?"

"Tell your friends they're to back away until I tell them to stop."

"This will avail you nothing, dear lady."

"Tell them."

Sacripant obeyed. Some of the Bloods balked until Three Bulls spoke harshly.

Winona let them go a good ten yards before she said, "That's far enough." To Nate she said without looking at him. "Our horses."

Nate was already on his feet. Bright Rainbow went with him, holding fast to his hand. "Let go," he said in Shoshone, but when he tried to raise his arm, she clung on. "Please," he said, but she still held fast, staring in fright at the Bloods.

Winona hadn't taken her eyes off Sacripant. She heard Nate and realized Bright Rainbow would hinder him. "Come to me, Bright Rainbow," she called out. "Quickly."

The girl instantly let go of Nate and ran over and wrapped her arms around Winona's waist.

Sacripant chuckled. "Most touching, eh? The child thinks you are her new *mere,* perhaps."

"Not a word out of you," Winona said. To let him distract her could prove disastrous. "Husband, quickly now."

Nate needed no urging. The Bloods might resort to their weapons at any moment and real blood would be spilled. He threw his saddle blanket and saddle on the bay and Winona's on the mare and finally saddled the dun. Upending the coffee pot, he shoved it into his parfleche and tied the parfleche on.

He'd overlooked the most important items of all; his own weapons. Moving swiftly, he collected his rifle and pistols and the bowie and tomahawk. He pointed the rifle at Three Bulls. "Translate for me, Sacripant."

"As you wish, *monsieur*," was the suave reply.

"Tell your friend that if he'd asked nice, I'd have tried to get the coup stick. I have no quarrel with him or his people."

Sacripant spoke in the Kainai language and Three Bulls replied. "Prove that you have no quarrel," he translated. "Leave your woman with us."

Rankled by the other's arrogance, Nate said, "No man worthy of the name would abandon his wife. Stay away from us, you hear, or the next time I'll shoot you on sight."

Winona, meanwhile, had backed away from Sacripant while holding her flintlock pointed at his face. She bumped against her mare, reached up without looking, and climbed on. "Now you, Bright Rainbow." She reached down without taking her gaze from the voyageur.

"My compliments, *jolie femme*," Sacripant said. "You are most crafty."

"Head west," Nate directed, and when Winona went past, he swung onto the bay while still pointing his rifle. "If you know what's good for you and your friend, this ends now."

"It ends when *we* say it does." Sacripant gave a little wave. "We will meet again, Grizzly Killer, and soon.

You can count on it."

CHAPTER FOURTEEN

Fester was so mad he could spit nails. The newest indignity was more than he could bear.

It started when Morton Thrack made a spectacular shot. They were moving through a belt of pines and spooked a grouse. Faster than Fester could blink, Thrack drew a pistol and fired.

It took considerable skill to drop a grouse on the wing. Fester was astounded when blood sprayed and the bird crashed to earth.

El Gato laughed and climbed down and picked the bird up. "*Magnifico!*" he exclaimed. "Right through the heart. You and I will have it for our next meal, *amigo.*"

"What about the rest of us?" Pedro asked.

"Shoot your own grouse," El Gato told him, and laughed louder.

Fester didn't think much more of it until along about noon when they stopped. El Gato tossed the grouse to Sabino and instructed him to pluck it.

Fester wanted to stretch his legs but a bandit made him sit. His wrists were still bound and he turned to Morton Thrack and shook them and said, "How about untyin' me? I can hardly feel my fingers."

"No."

"I promise I won't try and run off."

"No," Thrack said again.

"Have a heart. What harm can it do?"

"Ask me again and I'll pistol-whip you."

That shut Fester up. He fell into a sulk and hardly noticed when Pedro got a fire going and Sabino cut up the grouse. Nor did he pay much attention when a spit was rigged. The aroma, though, set his stomach to grumbling.

Presently El Gato tore off a piece and chewed lustily. "It is about done," he said.

"I wouldn't mind havin' me some of that there bird," Fester remarked, knowing full well they wouldn't give him any.

El Gato looked at him strangely. "You know, *gringo*, that isn't a bad idea. You should have part of it."

Fester was considerably surprised. "A leg would be nice." The prospect set his mouth to watering.

"Oh, you should have more than a leg," El Gato said. "Be patient."

Fester was tickled. He hadn't expected such generosity. "That's damned decent of you."

"Isn't it?" El Gato said, and laughed.

Morton Thrack sat and helped himself to some of the meat. No one else did. They weren't happy about being denied but they didn't complain. The memory of Alvarez was too fresh.

Fester mulled how to escape. Another jagged rock would help but they kept so close an eye on him, he couldn't pick one up without them noticing. He'd outfox them yet, somehow. Next time he'd steal a horse and ride like hell for Bent's, and take Marabell.

Fester was still mulling when El Gato got done eating, smacked his lips, and wiped his fingers on his pants.

El Gato snapped at several of his men in Spanish and they drew their knives and went off into the pines.

Fester idly wondered what they were up to. They were gone a long while. When they returned, one of the men carried a goodly size curved slab of bark. The man set it in front of El Gato and Fester saw that they'd used the bark like a bowl and there was something in it. At first he thought it was water but then he looked closer and saw that no, it was something else. He didn't recognize what until El Gato picked up a stick and stuck the end in the bark bowl. When El Gato raised the stick, a gooey substance clung to the end. It was pine tree sap.

Fester couldn't imagine what El Gato intended to do with it. He was taken aback when El Gato looked over at him and smiled.

"I promised you part of the grouse, si?"

"You ate all the meat, you damn hog," Fester said.

"I never said anything about meat, *gringo*," El Gato replied. He barked in Spanish.

Suddenly four bandits were on Fester. He squawked in anger as they seized him and held him down. Yet another began to untie his wrists.

"What is this?" he demanded. "What in hell do you think you're doin'?"

They were grinning and chuckling.

Fester's alarm grew when they commenced to remove his shirt. He swore and struggled but there were too many.

El Gato came over, carrying the bark bowl. Squatting, he swirled the stick in the sap, then sniffed it. "This smells good, yes?" He held the end of the stick under Fester's nose.

The pine scent was indeed pleasant but Fester was in no mood to appreciate it. "Let go of me, damn your hides. And give my shirt back."

"Soon you will have no need of one," El Gato said.

To Fester amazement, the bandit dipped the stick in the sap again and set to smearing the sap on his chest. "What the hell?"

Bandits were cackling.

Fester renewed his struggles, in vain. Tears of frustration filled his eyes as El Gato methodically applied the sap. He hated the cold, sticky feel. Once it dried it would be next to impossible to get off.

"This makes no sense," he said at one point. "Stop it, you hear?"

"Cluck for me," El Gato said.

"What?"

"Cluck for me like a chicken."

"Go to hell."

They sat Fester up and turned him so that El Gato could smear sap on his sides and his back. Fester was humiliated. He stopped resisting.

At last the bark bowl was empty. El Gato threw it aside, examined Fester, and grunted. He rattled off more Spanish.

Fester couldn't see what they were doing. He half-heartedly attempted to free his arms "Are you pleased with yourself?" he sarcastically asked.

"Very pleased," El Gato said. "*Usted hara un pollo hermoso.*"

"What's that mean?"

"You will see in a bit."

Pedro and Sabino came over.

When Fester saw what they had in their hands, he went rigid with shock. "No!"

"*Si*," El Gato said, his beady eyes twinkling with delight. "I told you that God and I are alike. Now I will prove it. As He did in the Garden of Eden, I will create an animal before your very eyes."

Fester found the strength to renew his impotent struggles.

The bandits chortled and smirked, amused as much by his antics as by what El Gato was doing.

Careful not to touch the sap with his fingers, El Gato applied grouse feathers to Fester's scrawny torso. There were so many that when the final one was pressed to the sap, Fester was practically covered from his neck to his waist.

Roaring with mirth, the bandits let go.

El Gato rose and took a step back and appraised his handwork. "*Magnifico*. All you need is a beak and wings and you could lay eggs."

One of the bandits doubled over with his hands on his knees, he was laughing so hard.

Fester stared down at himself, and could have cried. He fought an impulse to rip the feathers off. He'd only get sap all over his hands. "You are plumb *loco*."

"My little chicken," El Gato said, grinning and patting Fester's head. "You look so good, we should cook you and eat you." At that, he laughed until his big belly shook. When he finally stopped, he asked between gasps of breath, "Nothing more to say, my wonderful work of art?"

"I wish you were dead," Fester said.

CHAPTER FIFTEEN

Nate had a high regard for horses and never mistreated them if he could help it. He'd never ridden one into the ground. But he nearly did now. He pushed their animals to the point of exhaustion.

Winona had always admired her husband's high regard for life of all kinds. He never killed anything without cause, unlike some who shot things for the 'fun of it', as they were fond of saying. Nate brought down game for the supper pot, or if they needed a hide for clothing. But otherwise he treated wildlife with a respect much like that of her own people. She knew how unusual it was for him to drive their horses so hard. And she understood why.

For half the day they rode and rode, stopping infrequently and then only long enough to turn in their saddles and scan their back trail.

The sun was on its afternoon arc when they stopped once more.

"Nothing," Nate said, scouring the forest in their wake. "You?"

"Not a trace," Winona said.

"They should have shown by now."

Winona shrugged. "Maybe it took them longer than you think to find their horses."

Nate had scattered the Blood horses before he lit out

after Winona. Lead and a few arrows were sent his way but he had bent low over his horse and he wasn't hit.

"Or maybe they decided we're not worth the bother."

"We got the better of them," Nate said. "They can't live with that."

"Not can't," Winona said. "Won't." To most warriors, Shoshone and otherwise, their pride came before all else.

Bright Rainbow had stayed silent all morning. Now she raised her head and said matter-of-factly. "When they catch us they will be mad."

"If they catch us," Winona amended.

"Let's keep going," Nate said, and used his heels on the bay.

The countryside changed as they descended from mountainous terrain to a tableland that stretched for miles.

The next time Nate glanced back, he happened to notice Bright Rainbow staring at him. It triggered a thought, and about an hour later, when they drew rein, he turned in his saddle and said, "Bright Rainbow?"

"Yes, Grizzly Killer," she timidly answered in the same small voice she always did when she talked to him.

"Your people know that the Bloods are looking for them?"

"Yes."

"And they know that all the Bloods want is Spotted Wolf's coup stick?"

"My father said they know that, yes."

"Then why in hell—-," Nate began in English. Catching himself, he said more calmly in Shoshone,

"Why don't they give it to them?"

"The coup stick is ours now. Spotted Wolf's horse is ours. His bow is ours. His knife is ours."

"The Bloods don't care about the horse or the bow or any of that. All Three Bulls wants is the coup stick. If your people give it to him, he and the other Bloods will go back to their village."

"My father said we can not do that," Bright Rainbow reiterated.

"Your people aren't war-like. They don't go on raids. And they never count coup," Nate said, growing a trifle angry. "What use is the stick to them?"

"My father said—-."

Nate cut her off with a gesture while saying to Winona, "Did you hear that nonsense?"

"I am right here," Winona said.

"I've heard of some stupid stunts in my time but this beats all." Nate scowled. "The Tukaduka risk going to war with one of the most powerful tribes on the frontier over a stick they don't have any use for. Does that make sense to you?"

"They must have a reason we can not think of."

"Besides being stupid?"

"Why are you so mad?"

"Because we wouldn't be running from the damn Bloods if the Tukadukas weren't so pigheaded."

"You are swearing a lot today."

"Sorry"

"You are taking this too personal."

"I sure am," Nate said. "Look at our horses. They're on their last legs thanks to the idiot Sheepeaters."

"Be nice, husband."

"Grizzly Killer?" Bright Rainbow said.

Nate was still talking to Winona. "Why don't they get the Apaches mad at them while they're at it?"

"You're being silly."

"The Comanches, too, so they can be wiped out that much sooner?"

"Grizzly Killer?" Bright Rainbow said again.

"What?" Nate inadvertently snapped.

Bright Rainbow pointed back the way they had come. "The Bloods are after us."

CHAPTER SIXTEEN

There they were, about a mile back, raising a little dust.

Nate reckoned that the Blood animals had to be just as tired as theirs, and pushed on. The issue would be decided by whoever's horses gave out first.

Every now and again Winona would feel Bright Rainbow tremble. The girl must be scared to death, she realized. Winona couldn't do much to comfort her while they were in the saddle except to say at one point. "Don't worry. We won't let them get their hands on you." She wished that she felt as confident as she tried to sound.

The woods thinned and rolling grassland unfolded, broken by scattered rock outcroppings.

When they came on a small hill, Nate veered toward it. On the west side he drew rein and dismounted and led the bay into a cluster of large boulders where it would be safe from arrows and bullets.

Winona followed his example. She knew him as well as she knew herself and had divined his intention. "We make a stand?"

"We do," Nate replied. Untying his parfleche, he swung it over his shoulder. He also grabbed their water skin.

A ring of boulders topped the hill. In the middle was

a flat space more than wide enough for the three of them to sit and wait.

Nate checked his rifle and his pistols. He adjusted the straps to his powder horn and ammunition pouch so they were in easy reach. Leaning back, he rubbed his eyes.

Winona peered out. The Bloods were still after them, wisely holding their tired animals to a walk. It would be a while before they got within range. "Would you like something to eat?" she asked Bright Rainbow.

Nate took that as a hint and opened his parfleche. He laid out the bundle of pemmican and helped himself to a piece.

"Thank you," Bright Rainbow said in Shoshone.

Nate opened the water skin. He offered it to Winona and after she drank she held it for Bright Rainbow. Nate's throat was dry but he only took a few sips. They might need the water more later on.

Winona saw to her weapons, saying with a grin, "We sure get into some fixes, don't we?"

"It's living in the wild," Nate said. Constantly unpredictable, constantly dangerous, they never knew but when they might step out their cabin door and be confronted by a grizzly or a black bear or a rattlesnake. They never knew but when hostiles would swoop down on their valley.

Balanced against the many perils were the good days, or the glorious days, as Nate liked to think of them. Days when all was right with the world. When nothing bad happened, and their valley was serene. He liked those days best. Were it up to him, there wouldn't be any bad days. But that was a dreamer's fancy. The real world wasn't like that. Good and bad were part and parcel of things.

Truth to tell, Nate reflected, the bad days made the good days more enjoyable. Good days were like good wine or good brandy; every minute, like every sip, should be savored.

Nate grinned wryly, and shook his head. Here they were, about to tangle with a Blood war party, and he was thinking about life's inequities. He supposed that was what came from being a reader.

For some reason Nate thought of his copy of *Frankenstein* and had a desire to read it again.

The rumble of hooves brought him out of himself.

The Bloods had closed to within five hundred yards. In the lead was a warrior with his face bent to the ground. Their best tracker, was Nate's guess.

"They don't know we're here," Winona said quietly. Not that she needed to. The Bloods couldn't hear her that far out.

Nate wedged his Hawken to his shoulder. Sighting down the barrel, he curled his thumb around the hammer.

"The horse or the man?" Winona asked, although she knew what he would say.

"The horse." Nate wanted to avert spilling blood. Human blood, anyway. As much as it went against his grain, he reasoned that killing a few of their mounts might persuade the Bloods to leave them be.

"Do you want me to shoot a horse too?"

"Sacripant's."

Winona smiled. "With pleasure."

Nate thumbed back the hammer. He pulled the rear

trigger to set the front trigger and moved his trigger finger from the rear to the front but didn't squeeze. Not yet. They weren't quite near enough.

"I would like to see the look on Sacripant's face," Winona said.

"He rubs you the wrong way, I take it?"

"It's his eyes. They devour me."

"Then shoot him instead of his horse," Nate said, only partly in jest.

Suddenly the tracker glanced up and brought his horse to a halt. He stared intently at the ring of boulders and raised an arm to signal those behind him to stop.

Nate wondered if the gleam of sunlight on their barrels had given them away. He raised his cheek from the Hawken and saw that Bright Rainbow had stood and moved to a gap and was standing in plain sight. "The girl," he said.

Winona looked around. "Bright Rainbow!" she exclaimed. Grabbing the child's wrist, she pulled her back. "What are you thinking? They saw you."

Nate put his cheek back on the Hawken. The Bloods were talking among themselves. Any moment, they would fan out. Holding his breath, he steadied the rifle. It was a long shot, longer than any he'd attempted. When he was as sure as he could be, he smoothly stroked the trigger. Smoke belched from the muzzle and there was the loud crack. For a few moments he thought he'd missed.

Then the tracker's horse reared and whinnied and crashed onto its side.

Winona took hasty aim. In the second or two she

had taken her eyes off of Sacripant to glance at Bright Rainbow, the breed's horse had moved a couple of steps to the left. She compensated, raised her barrel slightly because of the range, and fired.

The Bloods were breaking for cover. Sacripant was hauling on his reins, and suddenly his horse stumbled and its front legs buckled. He pitched forward, clutched at its mane, and fell headlong to earth.

Nate reloaded as fast as his fingers could fly. He'd done it so many times over the years that he could do it with his eyes closed. He opened the powder horn and poured the right amount of powder into his palm, then fed the powder down the barrel. Next he took a ball and patch from his ammo pouch and wrapped the ball in the patch. Yanking the ramrod from its housing. he tamped the ball and the patch down.

Winona was reloading, too. She saw Sacripant rise unsteadily. Three Bulls came to his aid. Reining over and bending, the warrior swung the breed up behind him and they raced after their companions. Sacripant's horse was thrashing and neighing; she had missed its vitals.

Nate raised his Hawken but the Bloods were out of range.

The warriors stopped and one of them raised a fist and shook it. Dismounting, they huddled.

"The fat's in the fire now," he said.

Winona's conscience pricked her. She wasn't squeamish but she didn't like for anything to suffer and Sacripant's horse was in agony. "Do we run for it or stay put?"

Nate was inclined to light a shuck but their horses

were worn out. They wouldn't get far before the Bloods overtook them, and out in the open they stood no prayer at all. "I vote we stay put for the time being."

"I think the same." Winona raised her rifle. "I'm going to put that horse out of its misery."

"Want me to?" Nate asked. She was better with languages but he was a better shot.

"Would you?"

Nate aimed with care. When he fired, he hoped to see the downed horse collapse. Instead, it went into convulsions and whinnied stridently. "Consarn it."

"You hit it. I am sure."

Angry yells rose from the Bloods and more fists were shaken.

"Things have changed," Winona said.

"How so?" Nate asked as he poured black powder down his barrel.

"The Bloods are out for *our* blood."

CHAPTER SEVENTEEN

Nate wasn't so sure. It depended on how badly Three Bulls wanted his father's coup stick. He finished reloading and once again went through the ritual of aiming and holding his breath and setting the front trigger.

The stricken horse was whinnying and raising and lowering its head. The next time it raised up, Nate fired. Scarlet sprayed, and the horse thrust its legs out, uttered a last, piercing whinny, and died.

"Thank you," Winona said.

Nate reloaded. Leaning against a boulder, he set the Hawken across his legs. For the time being they were safe.

Winona turned to Bright Rainbow. The girl's fingers were dug into the dirt so hard, her knuckles were white, and tears filmed her eyes. "Are you all right, little one?"

"I do not want you to die."

Winona touched Bright Rainbow's chin. "I am not dead yet," she said with a smile.

"If you leave me you can get away."

"No."

"I slow you down. I do stupid things. Without me, the two of you can escape."

"We will never desert you. You are our friend."

Bright Rainbow sniffled. "I thought I was more than

that."

"Oh, child." Winona draped an arm over the girl's thin shoulders. "We have been all through this. If we could keep you, we would."

"I would love to be yours," Bright Rainbow said quietly. "I would cook and clean and do whatever you ask of me."

Winona kissed the top of the child's head and looked over at Nate.

"We came all this way to find her kin and that's what we should do."

"I suppose so," Winona said. She pulled Bright Rainbow to her and they hugged.

"I am sorry I am not good enough for you to keep me," the girl said.

"We have never thought that," Winona said. "You are a wonderful girl."

Bright Rainbow silently cried.

Nate felt sorry for her, but right was right. He concentrated on the Bloods. They were still huddled out there. He mentally crossed his fingers that they would mount up and ride off but that was wishful thinking. Before long they broke apart and moved off on foot into the grass, some to one side and some to the other, circling to surround the hill. One man was left to watch their horses.

Nate fingered his Hawken. He'd held off shooting the warriors but would shoot if they attacked. "This isn't good."

"What are they doing?" Winona asked softly. Bright Rainbow had fallen asleep in her arms.

"Fixing to rush us."

"How soon?"

"They'll likely wait until sunset," Nate guessed. He gazed westward, marking the position of the sun. "That gives us a couple of hours."

"By then the horses will be rested."

"I take your notion. Until then, one of us has to go down and keep an eye on them."

"You go," Winona said, indicating the sleeping girl. "I don't want to disturb her. I'll keep watch from up here."

Going over, Nate kissed Winona and tenderly touched her cheek. "Be careful."

"You as well."

Flattening, Nate snaked through a gap and down around more boulders until he reached the bay and the other horses. He didn't once show himself. The horses hardly reacted, they were so exhausted.

Nate hunkered with the Hawken's stock on the ground and his hands around the barrel. The waist-high grass rustled slightly from the breeze. Otherwise, the world around him was deceptively quiet.

To the west the sun dipped by gradual degrees until it was a blazing ball on the horizon.

Nate tensed. He'd heard a sound from off in the grass, a soft scrape. He rose a little higher. Twenty feet out the tops of the grass moved more than the breeze accounted for.

One of the Bloods was slinking toward their horses, intending to spook them or take them, no doubt.

Sinking flat, Nate curled the hammer back, and waited. The grass near him rustled. Fingers poked through the stems and parted them.

Nate took aim.

CHAPTER EIGHTEEN

It was Sacripant, his gaze locked on the horses. He didn't notice Nate until Nate said, "Have a nice crawl?"

To the halfbreed's credit, he didn't panic and try to bolt. He didn't show any fear at all. He looked at Nate in mild consternation, grinned, and said, "This is embarrassing, *mon ami*."

"I'm not your friend," Nate said, and wagged his rifle. "Suppose you ease on out here so I can see all of you. And keep your hands where I can see them."

"Go easy on that trigger, *s'il vous plait*. I have what you call a sweetheart and she is very fond of my face."

"There's no accounting for taste," Nate said.

Sacripant chuckled. "You have a fine sense of humor."

"Do you see me laughing?" Nate said.

Easing his other arm into view with his rifle flat on the ground, Sacripant emerged. "May I sit up?" he requested. "This is most undignified."

"What do you know of dignity?"

"Pettiness ill becomes you. May I sit up or not?"

"First you hand your rifle over," Nate commanded. "Then your pistol and your knife."

"Perhaps my moccasins while I am at it?" Sacripant said.

"Keep your voice down."

"*Oui. Desole.*"

Nate grabbed the rifle and set it behind him. He did the same with the breed's other weapons. "All right. You can sit up. Do it slow."

"I am a turtle," Sacripant said. He draped his forearms over his knees and smiled his easy smile. "Your beautiful woman and the girl, they are above us, no?"

"You should keep that in mind," Nate said.

"Eh?"

"She's *my* beautiful woman, and I'll kill anyone who puts a hand on her."

Sacripant sighed. "Is there anything so unreasonable as a jealous husband?"

"Had trouble with some, have you?"

"My share," Sacripant admitted, and then must have realized the mistake he'd made. "But I have no interest in your wife, I assure you."

"You are full of it up to your ears."

"Full of what?" Sacripant said. It dawned on him and he went on, "Oh. That. Yes, your humor is most excellent."

"So is my aim."

"That reminds me. It was ungallant of you to shoot our horses. Black Badger is very mad. One of those you killed was his. He says we should skin you alive."

"I warned you to leave us be."

"And I was happy to do so. But the others do as Three Bulls wants, and he will not rest until he has his father's coup stick. He is obsessed, that one."

"He should send someone to the Tukadukas and offer to trade for it."

"How can he when they run like rabbits at the sight of us?"

"You can't blame them after what you did."

"I did not torture the one we caught. That was Three Bulls' doing. I advised against it, in fact."

"Noble through and through."

"Why do you persist in insulting me? I tell you true. I am far more kind than my friends."

"And elk fly."

Sacripant scowled. "Scoff, *mon ami*. But I am *en partie Francaise*, part French, yes? And while I spend some of each year with the Blood half of my family, I spend much time with my white family, too. I live in both worlds and am often looked down on by both."

Nate thought of Zach and the bigotry his son had endured, and was silent.

"I bring this up because while I am part Blood, I am not like them in all their ways. I do not count coup. I do not aspire to be a great warrior. I am not as sanguinary as Three Bulls."

"As what?"

"As bloodthirsty. I do not put it past him to kill you once you bring him the coup stick."

Nate was amazed. "You admit that he might?"

"I'm not a saint, *monsieur*. I have confessed my fondness for the *mesdames*, for the ladies, have I not?"

"Don't remind me."

Sacripant shifted. "So what now? Do you shoot me in cold blood?"

"I should." It was the smart thing to do, Nate told himself. Whittle the odds. But he couldn't. He never took life except in self-defense. "But you get to go on breathing so long as you do as I say."

"In that case, I prick my ears to your every word," Sacripant said, grinning.

The sun, Nate noted, was half gone. "Your friends have us surrounded, I take it?"

"They will not let you leave, I am afraid. I strongly suggest you give up. I can persuade Three Bulls to do as we originally intended."

"You keep my wife while I go after the coup stick?"

"*Oui*. And when you bring it to them, I will help you and your lovely wife escape."

"Sure you will," Nate said.

Sacripant poked at the dirt with a finger and said sadly, "I was afraid you wouldn't listen to reason but I had to try. It is why I showed myself to you."

"There you go pretending to be noble again," Nate said. "You were out to take our horses so we couldn't ride off."

"If that is what you care to believe. But no matter. Your fate is out of my hands." Sacripant looked into Nate's eyes. "You are already caught and don't realize it."

CHAPTER NINETEEN

Nate had Sacripant turn around. Drawing his Bowie, he cut whangs from his buckskins and tied them together. When he had a cord about ten inches long, he placed the Hawken in his lap, said, "Don't try anything," and tied Sacripant's wrists.

Sacripant was surprisingly docile. "Don't forget to do my ankles, as well."

"You're taking this better than I thought you would."

"What would you have me do? You have all my weapons."

Nate instructed the *voyageur* to lie on his side and tied his legs. "There." Gripping him by the shoulders, Nate dragged him past the bay to a boulder.

"Be careful he does not step on me."

"I wouldn't have taken you for yellow," Nate said.

"It's my face and my lady, remember?"

Nate stared.

"What?" Sacripant said.

Presently the sun sank and the blue sky faded to grey. Nate moved to where he could see the top of the hill. Winona's face appeared, and he beckoned.

Up above, Winona nodded. Taking Bright Rainbow's hand, she said, "It's time. We must stay low so the Bloods don't see us."

"Just so we are together."

Exercising caution, they worked down the slope. Winona saw no sign of their enemies. Suddenly her knee hit something so hard, she grit her teeth to keep from crying out. It was a rock partially imbedded in the ground. "Watch out," she whispered through clenched teeth, and pointed.

Bright Rainbow nodded.

Mindful of her guns, Winona went on crawling. She could feel unseen eyes on her and tried to tell herself it was nerves.

Nate was waiting, and helped her rise into a crouch.

Winona did the same for Bright Rainbow. She saw the girl's eyes widen, and spun. "You!" she blurted in surprise on seeing who was tied behind Nate.

"We meet again, fair one," Sacripant said, oozing charm. "Forgive me for not rising and kissing your hand, but as you can see, you husband doesn't trust me."

"Neither do I," Winona said.

"*Vous me percez le coeur*," Sacripant said, sounding stricken.

Winona placed her hand on the hilt of her knife. "Understand this. My husband is the only man who may touch me. Should you ever try, I will put an end to you and your lust."

"Lust? No, *madame. Amour.* It is my curse to feel it for every beautiful woman I meet."

His laugh was so infectious that Winona almost smiled.

Nate wasn't nearly as amused. Pressing the Hawken to Sacripant's chest, he said gruffly, "I warned you about that."

"*Oui.* But I can no more help being me than you can help being you."

"Gag him," Winona suggested.

"Glad to." Nate opened his parfleche and found a cloth he used to clean and oil his guns. A few slashes of his bowie and he had the strips he needed. He held one up.

Sacripant was horrified. "You intend to stick that filthy thing in my mouth?"

"I can use one of my socks if you want."

"The stink alone would kill me." Sacripant swore under his breath. "*Tres bien.* Go ahead. But know that I will hold this indignity against you."

"You're the one who doesn't know when to shut up."

Bright Rainbow was watching the high grass. She tugged on Winona's arm, and when Winona bent down, she whispered, "There is something out there."

Winona looked. The breeze had momentarily died and the grass wasn't moving. "I don't see anything."

"It's them," Bright Rainbow said.

Nate unfurled high enough to see over the grass. For as far as he could see, it was undisturbed. Crouching, he whispered, "I don't see them, either."

"The Bloods are out there," Bright Rainbow insisted.

Nate didn't doubt they were. He figured they were well back from the hill and spaced far apart. With a little luck, he and Winona could break out of the ring and be well away before the warriors gave chase. "As soon as it's dark enough, we'll mount up. I'll go last and cover you."

Winona would rather stay at his side but she had the

girl to think of. "Due west?"

"Like bats out of a cave."

The sky darkened. A few early stars speckled the gathering gloom and somewhere a fox keened.

"It's time," Nate announced.

Winona quickly climbed on her mare.

Nate swung Bright Rainbow on behind her and gave Winona the dun's reins. He smiled encouragement, then vaulted onto the bay.

Sacripant shook his head and made low sounds through the gag as if to dissuade them.

Nate pointed his Hawken at him and Sacripant fell silent. "Not a peep, you hear? I am done trying to be reasonable with you."

"Hold tight," Winona whispered to Bright Rainbow, and patted her.

"If something happens to me, you're not to stop," Nate said.

"Be serious."

"I was."

"How long have we been man and wife?" Winona rejoined. "You know me as well as I know myself. You know it is not in me to abandon my man, just as it is not in you to desert your woman. Our hearts are entwined forever."

Nate switched the reins to his left hand so his right was free to hold the Hawken. "Have I told you that I loved you lately?"

"Not in the past five minutes, no. But I never tire of hearing it."

"Let's ride like hell," Nate said.

"Such language," Winona said.

They exploded into motion.

CHAPTER TWENTY

A jab of Winona's heels and the mare came to a gallop. She yanked on the lead rope, plowing through the grass like a canoe through water.

Nate stayed right behind them, alert for movement. He caught a hint of it in the grass ahead but didn't have time to raise his rifle before figures heaved up in front of Winona. Her mare instinctively slowed, enabling the warriors to grab hold of the bridle.

The Bloods had outsmarted them. The warriors weren't ringing the hill. They'd closed in and had been biding their time.

A hand clutched at Winona's leg and she kicked it off. Another grabbed at her reins. She kicked again and heard a grunt of pain.

More Bloods reared, reaching out.

Bright Rainbow screamed.

Nate tried to help them. A warrior barred his way and he drove the Hawken's stock at the man's head. Another got hold of his foot. Nate swept the Hawken around and down and felt the jolt of the blow clear up to his shoulders.

Winona pointed her rifle and was wrapping her thumb around the hammer when the Hawken was wrenched from her grasp. She clawed for a flintlock, only to have her arm seized. She sought to pull free but she was torn from her saddle and flung to the earth. Her ribs spiked with pain. Sucking in a ragged breath, she made it to her knees.

A warrior loomed. He had a lance and drove the blunt end at her face.

Winona twisted, and was spared. Balling her fist, she hit him in the groin.

Nate saw the woman he loved fighting for her life, and lost control. His blood roaring in his veins, he launched himself from the saddle and slammed into a warrior about to grab Winona from behind. They both went down. Nate was up first, swinging the Hawken like a club. There was a crunch and the Blood sprawled flat.

Winona made it to her feet and turned toward the mare. She reached it and raised a moccasin, only to be sent flying by a blow she didn't see. She wound up on her back. A hand clamped on her right wrist. Another on her left. A knee pinned her chest. She bucked but the warrior was too heavy. She sought to claw his eyes but he was too strong. In desperation she slammed her forehead into his face.

Nate felt his left arm seized, and sent the Blood sprawling. Fingers wrapped around his throat and he lashed out with his fist. He took a step toward Winona, and was swarmed.

Bloods came at him from the right and the left, from the front and the back. He rammed the Hawken's muzzle into a gut, backhanded another foe. He punched. He kicked. Five were on him, a tide of sinew he couldn't resist. He was swept off his feet.

Winona broke free, only to have her legs swept from

under her. She did a somersault and smashed onto her shoulder. Had it been her head, she would have broken her neck. A warrior yelled and two more pounced.

Acutely aware of the stakes, Nate fought with frantic ferocity. He gave as good as he suffered, if not better, and he was on the verge of surging loose when his head seemed to cave in and the grass rushed up to meet him.

Winona's wrist was gripped. Her legs were pinned. She still had one arm free, and when a warrior attempted to grab it, she pummeled him about the neck. Another Blood lunged, and suddenly she was helpless.

Nate couldn't get his mind to work. The world spun and his stomach tried to crawl out his throat. Dimly, he felt his arms being jerked behind him. Voices in the Blood tongue filtered through.

Abruptly, Nate's senses were restored. His head pounded and his right shoulder throbbed. Dark forms blocked out most of the stars and something pricked him in the side. Swallowing to wet his throat, he croaked, "Winona?"

"I am here, husband."

"I'm sorry." Nate had underestimated the Bloods and paid dearly for his mistake.

"It is not your fault," Winona consoled him.

"It most certainly is," said a gay voice. "I warned him and I warned him but would he listen?"

Sacripant squatted beside Nate, his teeth white in the darkness. "I told you, *mon ami*, that you were as good as caught."

An awful insight dawned, and Nate felt more of a fool than ever. "You kept me talking while they snuck in close."

"I did," Sacripant said.

"Why didn't they just rush me?"

"You were well armed. And we already saw how good a shot you are. Some of us might have died. I decided it was better to wait for dark and let you ride into them."

"You sneaky bastard."

"*Merci pour le compliment.* But now I am afraid I have bad news."

"Your friends plan to torture us."

"Oh, no, *monsieur.* The bad news is not about you. It is about the little one. The girl."

Winona had been listening as she was being tied, and she struggled to sit up. "What about her?" she anxiously asked.

"She is gone," Sacripant said.

CHAPTER TWENTY-ONE

Winona's wrists were bound but her legs were free. She surged to her knees and was shoved back down. "Let me up," she demanded, and got her legs under her to try again. Sacripant said something, and this time the warriors didn't stop her. She ran a few steps and cast about in the well of darkness, calling Bright Rainbow's name. There was no reply.

Sacripant came over. "She must have fled during the fight, eh?"

"Where can she have gotten to?" Winona said in alarm. Bright Rainbow was a child, and alone, and there were so many dangers.

"We will camp here for tonight. Maybe when the child sees our fire and smells our food she will come back." Sacripant put his hand on her shoulder. "Do not worry, sweet one."

Winona shrugged his hand off. "Don't touch me."

"I beg your pardon," Sacripant said, "but I am only being friendly."

"I know better." Winona went to Nate. No one tried to stop her. She sat next to him and saw his expression and sensed he was in great pain. "How badly are you hurt?"

"I was hit over the noggin but I'm all right," Nate fibbed. His head was hammering so bad, he could hardly think.

Winona suspected he wasn't being honest with her. They had been together for so long and she knew him so well that his tone said more than his words. "You must rest."

"How can I?" Nate bobbed his head at the Bloods, and regretted it.

Sacripant materialized, a pistol in his hand. "To show you how kind I can be," he said to Winona, "I am sending most of my friends out to look for her."

"Thank you."

As soon as a fire was kindled, one of the Bloods went for the horses while the rest faded into the night.

Sacripant made Nate and Winona sit with their backs to a boulder while he roosted across from them, the pistol in his lap. "Well now," he said, holding his hands to the flames. "Isn't this nice?"

"Let us go," Winona said.

Sacripant chuckled. "Why would I want to do that, dear woman? We have you in our power and you will do as we say."

"That's just it," Winona said. "We've already offered to help you get the coup stick back. You don't have to do this."

"*Je suis desole*, but my friends do not trust you. They especially do not trust your husband. They have no great love for whites."

"He is as good a man as any ever born. When he gives his word, he keeps it," Winona said with deep pride.

"You are formidable in his defense. He is lucky to have you."

"I can talk for myself," Nate said. "I'll only give you my word if you free her as well as me."

Sacripant smiled. "We would never be so foolish. She is our, how you say, guarantee that you will do as we want."

"You'll pay for this."

"*S'il vous plait*, do not threaten me. We are grown men, are we not?"

Winona said, "They call him Grizzly Killer because he has killed many of the silver-tips. He is also like a bear in that he is slow to anger, but once he is mad, there is no stopping him."

"Spare me your bluster, if you please."

Steeling himself against the pain in his head, Nate bent toward the breed. "Listen to me. If you go through with this, if you keep my wife with you against her will, I will kill you. I will kill your friends. I will track you to the ends of the earth if need be and put all of you in your graves."

"Stop," Sacripant said. "This is silly. I am not a child to be scared by tough talk."

The word 'child' sent a spike of renewed anxiety through Winona. She gazed into the dark and heard a distant roar. "Bright Rainbow," she said softly.

"The girl is being as silly as your husband," Sacripant said. "We would not have harmed her."

"Her people fear you."

"The Kainai are feared by many."

At that they lapsed into silence and listened to a medley of animal cries.

Presently Sacripant cleared his throat. "It is taking them too long. I would have thought they would have found her by now."

"Maybe they won't find her at all," Winona worried.

"Should that be the case, it will make things a lot harder for your husband. With the girl at his side he could easily befriend the Tukadukas. Now they might run from him as they run from us and he will have no hope of obtaining the coup stick for us."

"What happens to me then?"

"You would be wise to learn the Kainai tongue," Sacripant said.

CHAPTER TWENTY-TWO

Fester Simmons wouldn't stop itching. It was the sap. It had caused him to break out in a rash, and then the itching commenced. He scratched and scratched but the sap had dried as hard as glue and he had to peel it off with his fingernails. It took forever. So far he had removed patches here and there but from the waist up he was still mostly sap and feathers.

Fester hated El Gato for what he'd done, hated him more than he ever hated anyone or anything in all his born days.

It didn't help that El Gato went on calling him his 'little chicken', or that the other bandits wouldn't stop laughing and snickering. Except for Mortan Thrack. Thrack hardly ever smiled, let alone laughed. Thrack scared Fester.

It was the dawn of a new day. Coffee was perking. Venison was being roasted on a spit, and Fester's stomach wouldn't stop growling. He sat glumly watching the bandits banter and joke and wished every damn one of them was dead.

"What is the matter, my little chicken?" El Gato said. "You look sad this fine morning."

"Go to hell."

El Gato laughed. "You are grumpy for a chicken. It is all this sitting around. You need something to do."

He grinned and snapped his fingers. "I have an idea. Why don't you practice how to cluck and peck at the dirt."

"Go to hell again," Fester said.

El Gato's features hardened. "It wasn't a request, gringo. Do as I say or you will be a dead *poco pollo.*"

Fester decided enough was enough. He didn't care if they killed him. He'd be damned if he'd peck in the dirt and squawk. He was about to say so when he was spared by the arrival of Pedro and Sabino, who came running into the clearing. They had been off gathering firewood, and now they pointed back the way they came and rattled at El Gato in Spanish.

El Gato rose and made off with them, Morton Thrack at his side. The rest stayed in camp.

Curious, Fester got up and followed. No one tried to stop him. He reckoned they didn't think he was much of a threat. He'd show them, sooner or later.

A wooded slope brought them to a rise. El Gato and the others flattened and crawled to the top. Removing their sombreros, they peered over. Thrack kept his black hat on.

Fester dropped and crawled, too. He hoped it was white men. He'd give a holler and run to them for help. But when he raised his eyes high enough to see, he was disappointed. About a quarter of a mile below were some Indians. Even at that distance he pegged them as Tukadukas. They were on foot, for one thing. Most Indians had horses. For another, they didn't have much in the way of effects. He counted seven. It looked to be two men and two women and three sprouts.

"What tribe, do you think?" El Gato said to Thrack.

"Sheepeaters."

"They have herds of sheep?"

"Not those kind," Thrack said. "They hunt mountain sheep."

"What do they have that is valuable?"

Fester laughed and said, "You damned fool. They don't own a thing of any use to the likes of you. They're so poor, other tribes don't bother to raid them."

"Be careful with your insults, chicken," El Gato said. His brow puckered and he scratched his chin. "They must have something we can use. Everyone has something."

Without thinking Fester said, "I wouldn't, were I you. This time of year, there are hundreds of them hereabouts."

"Why would that be?"

"It's their big hunt," Fester said. "Once a year they come down out of the high country and have their grasshopper surrounds."

"Grasshoppers?" El Gato said.

"*Saltamontes*," Thrack said.

El Gato was amazed. "They eat them?"

Thrack nodded.

El Gato stared down the mountain. "Are all these Sheepeaters *loco*?"

"They eat what they can catch," Fester said. "They don't have horses so they can't go after buffalo."

"But to hunt grasshoppers," El Gato said in disgust. "What sort of people eat bugs?"

"What sort of people smear other people with sap and cover them with chicken feathers?"

"You amuse me less and less," El Gato said.

"Do we kill them?" Sabino asked in very poor English.

El Gato shook his head. "No. We let these go on their way. I must give more thought to these grasshopper eaters. They have to be of some use to us."

Fester trailed the bandits back to camp. The Tukadukas could be of use to him, too. He knew some of them. He was confident they'd help him if he asked. But first he had to get away from his captors.

El Gato sat, slid his knife from its sheath, and speared a piece of sizzling deer meat. He blew on it and took a bite and chewed lustily. "Where does this *saltamontes* hunt take place?" he asked, looking at Fester.

"Northeast of here, about a two day ride."

"Their women, are they *bastante*? Are they pretty?"

"Their men think so."

"Would *I* think so?" El Gato said. "Would my men think so?" He glanced at Thrack Morton. "What do you say?"

Thrack shrugged. "The young ones are, I reckon. The older ones are scrawny and as wrinkled as prunes."

El Gato grinned at the others. "How about it, *amigos*? Pedro? Sabino? Miguel? The rest of you? Should we help ourselves to some of their females? For myself, it has been a while, and I have missed the *chicas*."

"There will be hundreds of Indians," Pedro said. "That is too many, even for us."

"We will do it smart, like I do everything," El Gato assured him. "We have horses and they do not. We will take the women far away where the men can not catch us and have our way with them."

"And then?" Fester asked.

"What do you think, silly chicken? We will marry them and settle down and raise families." El Gato roared with mirth.

"What will you really do?" Fester pressed him.

"We will kill the bitches."

CHAPTER TWENTY-THREE

"Off you go, *mon ami*."

Nate King rubbed his chafed wrists and glared at Sacripant and the Bloods. Winona was on the other side of the fire, tied wrists and ankles.

"Don't," she said.

Sacripant shot a glance at her. "Don't what?" He looked at Nate, at Nate's eyes. "Be sensible, *monsieur*. We have given you ten days to find the Tukadukas and bring us the coup stick. Until then, you have my word that your woman will not come to harm."

"Your word isn't worth—-," Nate began, and stopped at a shake of Winona's head.

Sacripant smirked. "Your horse is waiting. Head due west and in a day or two you should be where the Sheepeaters usually gather."

"What if they're not there?" Nate had a litany of objections. "What if they hide from me like they hid from you? Or try to drive me off? Or catch me taking the coup stick?"

"You're a clever man, Grizzly Killer. You will think of a way to do it." Sacripant nodded at Winona. "Keep in mind what you will lose if you fail. That should be incentive, yes?"

"Cur," Nate said.

Frowning, Sacripant flicked the fingers of his right hand. "Off with you. I tire of your childishness." As if that reminded him of Bright Rainbow, he said, "It is a pity we couldn't find the girl. Without her as an excuse for seeking the Tukadukas, they will not be as friendly."

Nate hesitated. He couldn't bring himself to leave Winona. Then Three Bulls spoke harshly in the Blood tongue and pressed the tip of his lance to Winona's leg.

"He says if you do not leave right this moment," Sacripant translated, "she will limp the rest of her life."

Nate got out of there before he did something reckless. He stepped to the bay and hooked his foot in the stirrup. The saddle creaked under him as he swung on and raised the reins. His eyes met Winona's.

"Hurry back, husband."

"I will."

"*Oui*, hurry back," Sacripant said, "and you will do us both a favor. I want to go home. We have been at this weeks now, and I tire of it. I miss our own country."

It took every ounce of Nate's will to turn the bay and jab his heels. He looked back twice. Each time his gaze lingered on Winona.

Winona's heart sank. She watched Nate and the bay shrink with distance. Eventually they dwindled to specks and were swallowed by the forest.

"And now it is you and me," Sacripant said, and pursed his lips and winked.

"Lay a finger on me and I'll tear your throat out with my teeth."

"A she-wolf, eh? I like that you have fire in your blood." Sacripant chuckled, then addressed two Blood warriors who promptly mounted and trotted to the west.

"Where are they going?" Winona anxiously asked.

"To make sure your husband doesn't turn back." Sacripant sat and filled a cup with coffee. "*Voulez-vous?*" he said, holding it out to her. "I will have your hands freed."

Winona didn't care for any coffee but she answered, "I'd be grateful."

Sacripant addressed a warrior who squatted and pried at the knots. "This is a good start. We have ten days together, perhaps more."

"Perhaps less," Winona said.

"If your husband succeeds, you mean." Sacripant lowered his voice even though none of the Bloods spoke English. "I will be honest. Between you and me, *belle dame*, it is unlikely the Tukadukas will let him have the coup stick. He will have to steal it and they might not give him the chance. Either way, if he is not back in ten days, you have seen the last of him."

"I would die before I would let that be true."

"You love him that much?"

"I love him more than anything. We are as one, he and I. My heart and his heart are one."

"You are a *poetesse*," Sacripant said. "But I trust you are also practical. Should he fail to return, I sincerely doubt you will kill yourself. And that is the only way to prevent the inevitable."

"You're mistaken," Winona said. "There are other ways."

"Such as?"

Winona smiled.

"I see. *Tres feminin.*" Sacripant held out the tin cup.

"I believe you wanted this."

Winona sat up and cupped it in her hands. She took a few sips while gazing longingly after Nate, then glanced at her ankles. "How about my legs? Can I untie them too?"

"No."

"That's not very gentlemanly."

"I just told you we are not stupid."

"What if I give you my word I won't run off?"

"The romantic in me would like to believe you," Sacripant said, "but the realist in me can't."

"I like you less and less," Winona said flatly.

"I, on the other hand, like you more and more. You have spirit. You have beauty. You have intelligence." Sacripant sighed. "It is a pity you only give yourself to one man."

"Pig," Winona said.

"An innocent comment like that incites you?" Sacripant said in seeming surprise.

"Now which one of us thinks the other is stupid?" Winona countered. "Nothing about you is innocent. You are a wolf, but it is not prey for your supper pot that you hunt."

"*Touche*," Sacripant said. "And since you have seen through me, I will speak plainly." He leered at her. "Whether your husband comes back or not is of no consequence. I have decided I want to have you."

Winona glared.

Unfazed, Sacripant went on. "It might be tonight, it might be three nights from now. Whenever it is, I promise you, beautiful one, that you will experience pleasure such as you have never known."

"Over my dead body," Winona vowed.

CHAPTER TWENTY-FOUR

Nate had never been so torn in his life. Part of him was for turning around. Another part of him felt that if he did as the Bloods wanted, he could avert bloodshed.

Nate drew rein. He needed to think it through logically but his insides were in turmoil. What it boiled down to was that his every instinct warned him not to trust Sacripant. And if his instincts were right, then the coup stick was irrelevant.

Winona came before all else.

Nate raised the reins and started to turn the bay, and stopped. Dust was rising to the east. Not much, but dust didn't rise by itself, which suggested some of the Bloods were following him.

If he turned back, they'd spot him and ruin any hope he had of rescuing Winona.

Nate was caught between the proverbial rock and a hard place. Reluctantly, he rode on.

In twelve hours, more or less, the sun would set. He could wait for nightfall and then head back but by then he'd have gone so far that it would take most of the night to reach where he'd left them.

"What to do?" Nate said out loud, and came out of the woods into a meadow. He had been so deep in thought that he was startled to see five people suddenly rise and wheel toward him.

They were as surprised as he was. It was a family, a man and a woman and three children. The latter scampered behind their mother. The father snatched an arrow from a small quiver, notched it to his bow string, and raised the bow. He sighted down the arrow but didn't let it fly. He appeared curious and studied Nate and the bay with keen interest.

Only then did Nate realize which tribe they belonged to. "By God, you're Tukadukas."

The father tilted his head and lowered the bow a little. "Tukaduka," he repeated.

Nate switched to the Shoshone tongue, saying, "*Tsaangu beaichehku*," which was 'good morning'. "*Ne hainji-ha.*" Or 'I am a friend.'

The father lowered his bow even more and came closer. "How are you called?"

"I am Grizzly Killer. I am white but I have been adopted into the eastern Shoshone. My wife Wi-no-na is of their tribe."

"You are the white who kills the great bears?" the man said, sounding impressed. "I have heard of you."

Nate grinned at his stroke of luck. While the western and eastern Shoshones weren't much alike, they did speak essentially the same tongue, and now and then they mingled. When they did, it was common to talk about things of importance, and his joining the tribe merited mentioning. He was the only white the Shoshones ever adopted. "How are you called?"

"I am Squirrel Tail." The man pointed at the woman. "This is Rabbit Running, my wife, and these are my children."

The formal introductions dispensed with, Nate dismounted. The children peered from behind Rabbit Running, clearly afraid. He smiled to show he was friendly, then went on to relate how the Bloods were holding Winona as ransom for Spotted Wolf's coup stick, ending with, "I come to your people as a brother and a fellow Shoshone. I beg you to help me by letting me have the stick so I can save her."

Squirrel Tail had listened with rapt attention. Now he took the arrow from his bow string and slid it into his quiver. "This is a grave matter. It is not my decision to make. I will take you to our gathering and present you to our chiefs."

Nate grasped the man's hand and warmly shook it. "Thank you. How long will it take us to get there?"

"One sleep."

More good news. Nate climbed back on the bay and they headed out. He rode next to Squirrel Tail, with the family behind. Their snail's pace was a test of his patience.

"My people did not realize how important the coup stick is to the Bloods," Squirrel Tail remarked. "We do not use them."

"I know," Nate said.

"If we had known we would have done things differently."

"Different how?"

Squirrel Tail didn't answer. Instead he said, "We do not like to make war."

"I don't blame you," Nate said.

"War is bad. Those we care for die. There is fear and blood."

"I have long believed that peace is better than war," Nate said.

"All men should believe that. Then we could all live happily."

There was the Tukaduka philosophy in a nutshell, Nate reflected. They were a simple, peaceful people, not easily provoked. So unlike the tribes who extolled counting coup on their enemies. He admired them for that.

"I hope we can help you, Grizzly Killer. I feel very sorry for you."

"Thank you."

"For the Bloods to take your wife——." Squirrel Tail stopped. "My heart would break if anyone took Rabbit Running. She is everything to me. I would not want to live without her."

"Thank you for understanding. I hope your chiefs will understand, as well."

"They are wise men, and kind," Squirrel Tail said. "Even to strangers."

Nate felt more confident by the moment. It could well be that he'd have the coup stick and be back with Winona in two or three days.

"They will want to help you, I am sure," Squirrel Tail assured him.

"That is good to hear."

Squirrel Tail glanced up and said a strange thing. "But we can not always do as we want, can we? There are times when things over which we have no control do not let us."

"Are you saying they might not give me the coup stick?" Nate asked in alarm.

"I am saying," Squirrel Tail said, "that you must talk to them, and then you will know."

CHAPTER TWENTY-FIVE

From the moment El Gato announced his plan to take Tukaduka women captive, Fester schemed to thwart him. He liked the Tukadukas. They were kindly folk. But they'd fight if they had no choice, and Fester couldn't think of anything that would make them madder than hearing that some cutthroats were out to rape their women.

For half a day the bandits trailed the two families, careful to stay well back.

El Gato couldn't stop thinking of the treats in store. As they were riding along, he rubbed his hands in anticipation and asked, "Do you like women as much as I do, little chicken?"

Fester had been made to walk at the side of El Gato's horse. His feet were sore and he itched terribly because of the sap and he hated his captors more than ever. "I can live without them."

"That is the trouble with gringos. You have no passion."

"Passion, hell," Fester said.

"It is the poor food you eat. *Pimientos*, *tequila* and *frijoles*, that is what you should be eating."

"If it was up to you, we'd be wearin' *sombreros* and takin' *siestas*, too."

"You could learn a lot from my people, *si*."

"The only thing I've learned from you is that they make 'em as rotten south of the border as they do north of it."

El Gato drew rein. He stared at Fester, then slowly climbed down, slowly turned, and punched Fester in the face.

Fester staggered, caught himself, and put a hand to his throbbing cheek. "You son of a bitch."

"I think I have tired of you, chicken." El Gato drew a pistol, pointed it, and grinned. "I think I will blow your brains out."

Morton Thrack, who was behind them, remarked, "Shots carry awful far in these mountains."

"Eh?" El Gato said.

"The Tukadukas," Thrack said.

El Gato frowned. "They might hear?" He angrily jerked the pistol down. "You are a lucky little chicken. But don't be too happy. Your time will come, and soon." He jammed the pistol under his belt, climbed on his horse, and rode on.

Fester absently fell into step next to Thrack's horse. "You saved my life."

"Wasn't thinking of you," Thrack said.

"Ain't you ever cared about anything but yourself?"

"No."

"You must have cared for somebody. Your ma and pa. A brother or sister. Or maybe it was a dog or a cat you had as a kid."

"Give it up, old man," Thrack said. "My folks died when I was two. I was too young to care much. I was sent to live with an uncle who didn't want me but felt obliged to take me in. His wife didn't want me, either.

Their own kids hated me. My life was hell. He beat me. She made me do twice the chores of her own brood. And the kids did all sorts of things to make me miserable, things that only kids could think of."

"So you had it rough. A lot of people do."

"I had it rough until I was twelve. One night my uncle decided to beat me for forgetting to feed the pigs so I stuck a knife in him. His wife flew at me so I stuck the knife in her, too. The kids ran but I caught them and slit their damn throats. I've been on my own ever since."

"That's why you're so cold-hearted."

"I treat people like they deserve."

"You've never met any nice folks?"

"People are only nice when they want something, and I know what you want. To help you get away."

"You can't judge everybody by those kin of yours."

"The hell I can't. I've been most everywhere and seen most everything and human nature is the same everywhere. People are mean and spiteful and selfish."

"Hogwash. There's a heap of folks who are decent and kind. Quakers, for instance. Or nuns. Who ever heard of a mean nun? Ordinary folks, too, who don't ever hurt anybody."

"I've met a few like that," Thrack admitted. "But not enough to change me. I learned early on not to give a damn about anybody but me."

"You've never wanted a wife or kids?"

"What the hell for? So I could work my fingers to the bone to provide for a woman who'd nag me to death, and for kids who'd up and leave as soon as they were old enough?" Thrack gestured. "Where's your wife and kids, if they're so great?"

"I like bein' alone."

"You're a fine one to talk, then."

"I don't go around hurtin' people. You let those kin of yours sour you on life, and look at where it got you."

"No, *life* soured me on life." Morton Thrack leaned down and jabbed Fester hard. "Not one more word about me or by God I'll beat your head in with a rock. Just see if I don't." He smiled an icy smile. "The Tukakukas won't hear that." Gigging his horse, he rode ahead.

"I'm havin' a hell of a day," Fester said.

CHAPTER TWENTY-SIX

Winona had made up her mind that she was going to escape at the first opportunity. The problem was, the Bloods were being extra careful not to give her the chance. She was always bound and always under guard.

Often throughout the morning and afternoon Winona caught Sacripant staring at her with hunger in his eyes. She ignored him. When he tried to talk to her, she stayed silent. It seemed to amuse him.

The Bloods were indifferent. To them she was nothing. Once Three Bulls came over and stood staring down at her. Why, she couldn't say. She was relieved when he walked off. He had a fierce mien, and he had been fingering his knife.

She was so stiff and sore from lying on the ground for so long, and her wrists and ankles hurt so much, that as evening fell, she broke her silence. "How about untying me? I can't feel my hands or my feet."

"The lady speaks," Sacripant said, and laughed.

"Please," Winona said.

The *voyageur* walked around behind her and knelt. He touched her hair and her shoulder.

"The ropes," Winona said.

"*Oui.*"

Winona felt his fingers lightly brush her arm. She debated slamming her head into his face but settled for saying, "It would be quicker if you used a knife."

"*Oui*, but I might cut you. And we will have need of the ropes later."

The Bloods were sitting around talking. Several had gone off earlier and returned with a dead doe. Now the meat was in sections and large chunks were roasting over the fire.

"Smell that?" Sacripant said, sniffing. "It smells delicious, does it not?" He brushed her arm again. "Are you hungry, *ma cherie?*"

"What does that mean?"

"*Ma cherie?* It means 'my sweet'."

"I am not your sweet," Winona said. "I am not your anything."

"Until your husband returns you are whatever I want you to be."

Winona nearly lost her temper. Restraining herself, she reminded him, "You gave your word I wouldn't be harmed."

"What I have in mind does not hurt."

"You're despicable," Winona said.

"*Au contraire*. Were I as vile as you think, I would throw you down and force myself on you——."

"You would try," Winona broke in.

"——but I am too much the gentleman. I like romance with my conquests."

Winona's hands were free. She sat up and rubbed her wrists and swung her legs around in front of her. "I'll do my ankles myself."

"And I will graciously let you." Sacripant slid next to her.

"Don't sit so close."

Sacripant pursed his lips. "I would have a care, were I you. You forget that you are our captive. You do as we tell you, not the other way around."

"Not when it comes to *that*, I won't," Winona informed him.

"There you go again," Sacripant said, and sighed. "What will it take to convince you that you do not have a choice?"

"As the whites would say, like hell I don't."

Sacripant studied her. "I begin to think you would not make a good wife. You are too strong willed."

"My husband has never complained."

"Because you have him wrapped around your finger. But you can't wrap any of us."

Enough feeling had returned to her hands that Winona attacked the rope around her legs. The knots were so tight she had to pry and pry.

"My curse has been that I like women too much," Sacripant said. "I can't get enough of them. Even as a boy, I admired girls when other boys were more interested in fishing and hunting."

"Why are you telling me this?"

"I don't know. Perhaps I don't want you to despise me. Perhaps if you understand you will not be so difficult."

"I haven't begun to be difficult," Winona said. "Try to force yourself on me and you will find that out."

"May I compliment you on your excellent English?"

"Jump off a cliff."

Sacripant laughed. "Have your fun while you can. When I am ready it will happen and there is nothing you can do to stop it." Rising, he moved around the fire to his friends.

Winona smothered a wave of fear. She must stay strong, for Nate's sake as well as her own. She knew her man, knew he would go berserk if she were violated. It would make him reckless, and reckless often led to an early grave.

She stared into the flames and didn't realize someone else had come over until a hand appeared holding a plate-sized flat rock with sizzling morsels of deer meat. She glanced up.

It was Three Bulls. He motioned for her to take the food and said something in his own tongue.

Across the fire, Sacripant chortled. "What is it about you?"

"About me how?" Winona said, confused.

"That you attract men so. Three Bulls thinks you would make a good addition to his lodge."

"He can't be serious."

"Three Bulls doesn't joke. If he decides to make you his, your fate, as they say, is sealed."

"What about you?" Winona said. "I thought you wanted me for yourself."

"I do. I also like breathing. If Three Bulls wants you he can have you, with my blessing."

"It doesn't matter to him that I already have a husband?"

"Why should it? He already has two wives. You would be his third." Sacripant laughed. "His lodge will be crowded."

CHAPTER TWENTY-SEVEN

Nate King had always heard that the Tukadukas were among the poorest tribes. He didn't appreciate how poor until he arrived at the gathering.

Over a hundred families were assembled. Although whites called them Sheepeaters, only some lived high in the mountains where mountain sheep were found. Others lived lower down and survived on whatever game they could catch, plus their staple of roots, sunflower seeds and pine nuts.

Some wore hides made from mountain sheep. A few wore buckskins. Rabbits skins were more common. The men were partial to breechcloths, the women to a sort of apron woven from, of all things, sagebrush. Women were required to be covered; the Tukaduka believed that anyone who looked on a naked woman went blind.

Tukaduka weapons were mostly bows and knives. They were masters at fashioning snares to catch small game and nets to catch fish.

A lot of them---the ones who dwelled at lower elevations where mountain sheep weren't found--- carried pointed sticks which they used to dig roots.

Nate learned from Squirrel Tail that they had a great fear of the Utes. It seemed the Utes regularly took captives to sell in Mexico as slaves.

His presence caused a considerable stir. A crowd gathered, the men openly admiring his rifle and other weapons, the women too timid to come too near. The children were scared and behaved as if he were a giant who might devour them.

Like other tribes, the Tukaduka had leaders who were looked up to for their sagacity and devotion to their welfare. Squirrel Tail was in conference with them for quite a while. When he came back he brought upsetting news.

"They will talk to you about the coup stick but not until tomorrow night."

"Why do I have to wait?" Nate was anxious to return to Winona. "Didn't you tell them that the Bloods have my wife?"

"I did," Squirrel Tail confirmed. "Tomorrow is the first day of the hunt. They are busy with that now and will listen to your appeal after it is over."

Nate couldn't hide how mad he was. He turned away before he said something he'd regret.

"I am sorry, Grizzly Killer," Squirrel Tail said.

Nate smothered his frustration. He knew that Indians weren't like whites. They rarely rushed into anything.

At the moment, the Tukadukas were settling down to prepare their supper. Their fare varied. Some had roots and berries to eat. Others had rabbit or squirrel meat. One hunter had shot a deer and it was carved up and the meat passed around.

Nate shared his pemmican with Squirrel Tail's family. He wasn't very hungry, himself. He nibbled on a piece and drank a little water and that was it. All he could think of was Winona.

As he was nibbling several men approached and stared at him. He noticed that one carried a bow unlike the bows of the others. It was bigger and better made, and looked a lot like the bows used by the Bloods with Sacripant. It sparked him into asking, "Is that the bow that belonged to Spotted Wolf?"

Squirrel Tail confirmed that it was. Another Tukaduka had the Blood's knife, still another his tomahawk, yet another his lance. Spotted Wolf's clothes had been cut up and made into breechcloths and aprons.

"What about his horse?"

"We ate it," Squirrel Tail revealed. "It fed a great many."

Everyone stayed up late mingling and talking. They only got together like this once a year and made the most of it.

Nate kept to himself. When he finally turned in about midnight, he couldn't sleep. Worry gnawed at him like termites gnawing at wood. He tossed and turned and got up and paced and lay back down and did more tossing and turning.

Dawn broke clear and bright but there was nothing bright about Nate's spirits. He kindled a fire and put coffee on to brew. Before long the aroma drew a crowd.

Squirrel Tail brought three older men over and introduced them. One was called Yellow Badger, the second Chirping Sparrow. The third and the oldest was known as Pine Cone. "They are our leaders."

Nate thought this was his chance. "You have come to talk about the coup stick?"

"Tonight," Pine Cone said.

"Why not now?" Nate asked. "If you will give it to me, I can be on my way." When no one responded, he stressed, "I am worried about my wife. There is no telling what the Bloods will do to her."

"We are sorry for her and for you," Chirping Sparrow said sadly.

"We will talk about the coup stick tonight," Yellow Badger reiterated.

All three smiled serenely.

"Please," Nate said. "I don't want my wife to come to harm."

"Nor do we," Pine Cone said.

"Then help me."

The three leaders looked at one another and Chirping Sparrow said, "We have heard of you, Grizzly Killer. It is said you speak with a straight tongue, and that you know the ways of the red people. If that is so, we ask that you respect our wishes."

"All I want is the coup stick," Nate said in mounting exasperation. It was all he could do not to grab one of them and throttle him to shake some sense into the whole bunch.

"There is more to this than you are aware," Pine Cone said. "We must talk it over and decide how best to help."

"What's to decide? Just give the stick to me."

"We can't," Yellow Badger said.

"We don't have it," Flying Sparrow said.

"Who does?" Nate anxiously asked. "I'll ask them to give it to me."

Pine Cone said. "Be patient a while longer."

They smiled in that serene way they had and turned and walked off.

Nate could have shot them.

CHAPTER TWENTY-EIGHT

Hours earlier, Winona King struggled to catch some sleep. She lay curled on her side with her back to the fire and willed herself to relax but couldn't. She rolled onto her back. She faced the fire. She turned away from it again. Finally she gave up and lay gazing at the stars and thinking of Nate.

All the Bloods save one were asleep. Sacripant had turned in, too, much to her relief.

By white reckoning it was pushing two in the morning when Winona finally felt herself succumbing to exhaustion. She closed her eyes and was on the cusp of drifting off when something touched her hair.

Startled, she jerked her head up, thinking it might be Sacripant. But no, she glanced over her shoulder and he was still asleep. The sentry was by the fire, paying no attention to her.

Winona attributed the feeling of being touched to her overwrought nerves. Closing her eyes, she felt the welcome tug of slumber.

Once again she was on the verge of drifting off when she felt a slight….something…..on her hair. An insect, she thought. Rising on her elbows, she ran her bound hands over the side of her head but nothing was there.

Annoyed with herself, Winona sank down. She figured to lie there and not move until sleep finally claimed her. She watched the flickering firelight play over the boulders. Her lids grew heavy and she was about to close her eyes when a tiny pebble came flying out of the dark and struck her hair, bounced off, and landed next to her.

Winona grew excited. It must be Nate, she reasoned. He'd snuck back and was letting her know he was close by. She stared at the boulders, hoping he would show himself, and sure enough, a face materialized out of the blackest of the shadows and smiled at her.

But it wasn't her husband.

It was Bright Rainbow.

Winona glanced at the sentry to be sure he hadn't seen. When she turned back, Bright Rainbow was crawling toward her. Winona motioned for her to stop, and pointed at the warrior by the fire. Bright Rainbow looked at him, nodded that she understood, and retreated into the shadows.

Winona was delighted the girl was alive and unhurt. She remembered how Bright Rainbow had survived on her own after her father and mother were killed. The girl was resourceful, and tougher than she seemed.

Winona pondered. If she could knock the warrior out or kill him—-but no, not with her arms and legs tied. She could crawl over to the boulders—-but no, the warrior would see her. Frustrated, she closed her eyes, and sighed. Her fatigue was beginning to tell. She needed to sleep, but how could she, as worried as she was? She opened her eyes and felt a wave of hope.

The warrior's chin had dipped to his chest. He was asleep, his arms slack at his sides. His lance, which he had been leaning on, was on the ground.

Here was her chance. Easing onto her hands and knees, she moved toward the fire. She had to pass close to Three Bulls but his back was to her and he didn't stir.

Winona reached the lance. Carefully picking it up, she backed away. When she was safely past Sacripant, she set the lance down. The tip was stone, not metal. Obsidian, she thought. She turned it so the spearhead was edge-up, pinned the shaft with her knees, and pressed the rope binding her wrists to the edge.

Over by the fire, the sentry slumbered on.

The strands parted but not fast enough to suit her. She pressed harder. A warrior mumbled in his sleep and turned over, and she froze. He smacked his lips, mumbled some more, and set to snoring.

Winona went on cutting. The slight scritch-scritch-scritch as she moved her wrists back and forth were, to her ears, thunderous. But none of the Bloods woke up.

She was already thinking ahead. If she got free, if Bright Rainbow was watching and came when she beckoned, if she could spirit their horses away—-if, if, if.

Another Blood moved but didn't open his eyes.

Winona felt a sharp sting, and jerked her wrists up. She'd cut herself. She needed to watch what she was doing. She bunched her shoulders, pressed down harder, and more strands gave way. She was almost through.

Winona would like to see Sacripant's face in the morning when he woke up and she wasn't there. She glanced over at him, and a fist of ice closed around her heart.

Sacripant had a pistol in his hand and glitters of

amusement in his dark eyes.

"What do you think you are doing, sweet one?"

Winona stopped cutting.

"You have been very naughty." Sacripant sat up. "And now you must be punished."

CHAPTER TWENTY-NINE

The Tukadukas were in fine spirits.

The grasshopper hunt was a high point of their year. Breakfasts were quickly attended to and everyone gathered around their leaders. Pine Cone gave a speech that brought a lot of smiles and laughter. Then about half the men split off and hurried away.

Despite himself, Nate was curious, and since Squirrel Tail was included, he tagged along.

The men hiked in single file for half a mile to a short plain. Some had sharp sticks. Others had long, jagged rocks. The use they would be put to was soon revealed.

Nate had noticed a few grasshoppers at the encampment. Here on the plain, they were everywhere.

The men filed out to the middle and about twenty of them began to dig. Sticks and rocks and dirt flew. When a man tired, he stepped back and was replaced by another. In a remarkably short time they had excavated a pit about twelve feet across and five feet deep. The dirt was spread around and tramped with their feet.

"What is the pit for?" Nate asked Squirrel Tail when his turn to dig ended.

"You will soon see," Squirrel Tail answered with a grin of anticipation.

They returned to the encampment.

Everyone was excited. There was a lot of milling and talking.

Then Pine Cone raised his arms for silence. "My children," he began, "today we feast. Today we share and show our love for one another and tonight we sleep with full bellies." He motioned. "Now hurry to your tasks. You know what to do. We must be in position when the sun is at its warmest."

Nate followed Squirrel Tail and the rest of the men into the woods where they spent half an hour gathering fallen tree limbs and climbing into trees and breaking other limbs off.

The women were waiting for them when they came out of the forest. Each woman held a basket. So did many of the older children.

Everyone made for the plain. There, the men broke up, forming into two long lines. One line filed to the north and then east, the other to the south and then west. Eventually the two ends met, enclosing a wide area of the plain---and the pit.

At a shout from Pine Cone, the men beat the ground with the tree limbs and slowly advanced. Grasshoppers by the hundreds leaped and took wing. Some of the grasshoppers tried to get through the line but the men were spaced so close together that most were driven back.

To Nate it was eerie, seeing thick clouds of swarming grasshoppers, and the ground covered inches deep. There was a continuous buzz of thousands of wings.

The men had perfected a technique for herding the hoppers. They'd move forward a short way, stop while the grasshoppers settled, then beat the ground and advance again.

In due course the line had closed to encompass about an acre. Inside it, an untold host of grasshoppers crawled over one another in a writhing mass yards deep.

The circle of men contracted. The mass of grasshoppers became thicker. With nowhere else to go, most of the grasshoppers retreated into the pit, exactly as the Tukadukas wanted.

Nate marveled at the result. The pit became filled to overflowing. At which point the men placed their branches upright, side by side, in effect forming a fence to keep the grasshoppers in.

At a yell from Pine Cone, the women and older children with baskets rushed forward. The men parted for them to slip through, and there followed a scene that never in Nate's wildest imagining would he have conceived.

The women and older children fell on the grasshoppers like starved wolves on tiny sheep. In a mad melee, they scooped, grabbed and flung grasshoppers into their baskets. It incited those in the pit to rise in a tide and seek to get away but the men with the branches battered them back.

Everyone was covered with grasshoppers. Crawling with grasshoppers. Practically breathing grasshoppers. But that didn't deter them. As soon as a basket was crammed full, a top was pressed over it and a new basket was passed in from others waiting outside the human fence. And through it all, the Tukadukas laughed and joked and had the grandest time.

Nate caught himself chuckling. He was sometimes

inclined to think that human beings were the most ridiculous creatures on the planet, and here was a good example of why. But it sure looked like fun.

A woman rose out of the pit, every inch of her covered with grasshoppers so that only her eyes showed. Another woman slipped on the gore of those inadvertently crushed, and upended, spilling her basket. A winged grasshopper flew into a girl's mouth and she gagged and coughed until another girl clapped her on the back.

On and on it went, until every basket was full.

Nate was so immersed in the spectacle that for a time he forgot about Winona. He was reminded when he saw a man and a woman kiss. Mad at himself, he clenched his fists.

Here he was, being amused by the Tukadukas' antics, while his wife was in grave peril. Enough was enough. He wasn't going to wait any longer. These people were going to tell him where the coup stick was or there would be hell to pay.

CHAPTER THIRTY

Three Tukaduka women were picking berries at the edge of a meadow. They had no notion that unseen eyes hungrily watched their every move.

Fester's first inclination was to shout and warn them. But El Gato would likely shoot him if he did, or worse, and while he didn't want to see the women harmed, he wasn't hankering to die. He might be getting on in years and not have a lot left but he wasn't ready to be put under.

So Fester crouched behind a fir and peered down at the women, as the rest of the bandits were doing, and stayed silent.

El Gato licked his lips. "*Mujeres bonitas*, eh?" he whispered to Sabino and Pedro.

Pedro beamed and said something in Spanish that made the other bandits grin and chuckle.

El Gato pointed at five of them and motioned at the females and the five crept off.

Now was his chance, Fester thought. El Gato was intent on the women and wouldn't spot him backing away. He'd only taken a few steps, though, when something gouged him in the back.

"Going somewhere, you old goat?" Mortan Thrack asked.

"Not me," Fester said.

Thrack came around from behind him holding a cocked flintlock. "I'll keep you company a spell."

"Lucky me."

"No, Thrack said, "your luck has about played out. You heard El Gato. He's tired of you. If I were a betting man, I'd bet you won't live out the night."

"Hell," Fester said.

"You didn't see this coming? Did you think you'd be his little chicken forever?"

Fester scratched at the feathers on his chest and didn't reply.

"As it is," Thrack said, "you've stayed alive longer than anyone else ever has. He really took a shine to you."

"I'd just as soon he hadn't."

"Then you'd already be dead." Thrack stared at the women, half-turning his back to Fester. "Who knows? He might go easy on you and make it quick."

"That's easy?"

"The hard way is for him to carve on you for an hour or two. And he does love to carve. Sometimes he gets so carried away, you'd think he has Apache blood in him."

Fester had a terrible thought. Terrible because it could get him killed. He cast about and spied a downed tree limb within easy reach. It lay in pieces, the biggest as thick his arm. Quietly as could be, he picked it up. He was half afraid the wood would be rotten but it hadn't been on the ground all that long. Clutching it in both hands, dazzled by his own grit, he raised it over his head.

Fester glanced around. Near as he could tell, none

of the other bandits were anywhere near. Tensing, he raised the club.

"Do you want to die now instead of later?" Thrack asked without turning.

Fester hesitated.

"Look at my left arm."

Perplexed, Fester did. "All I see is your shirt sleeve."

"Under the arm."

"Under it?" Fester did, and his skin crawled. He'd almost made the last blunder of his life. The muzzle of Thrack's flintlock was trained on him from under the killer's armpit. "How on earth?" he blurted in astonishment.

Lowering the pistol, Morton Thrack turned. "Look closer."

Flintlocks came in different designs. Some were plain and had little metal besides the hammer, the frizzen, the pan and the trigger. This particular pistol also had a wide metal band around the barrel, a band polished to a sheen so that it resembled a mirror.

Fester saw his reflection as plain as anything. "I'll be damnned."

Thrack hit him.

The blow rocked Fester onto his heels. He dropped the branch and tottered and would have fallen if he hadn't stumbled against a fir. For a few seconds the forest spun and wet drops trickled down his temple.

"The only reason you're still breathing," Morton Thrack said, "is that El Gato wants to kill you himself."

Fester's vision cleared but his legs were wobbly. "You can't blame a man for tryin'."

"Yes," Thrack said, "I can." He slid the pistol under

his belt. "Stay where you are until I say otherwise. Understand?"

"I'll pretend I'm a rock," Fester said.

"You already are between the ears."

Fester bristled at the insult but held his tongue.

Down the mountain, the bandits were almost to their quarry. The women talked and smiled in ignorant oblivion.

At a gesture from El Gato, the five bandits rushed them.

Fester hoped the women would scream so their cries would bring rescuers but they were so terror-struck, the bandits had hands over their mouths before they could utter a peep.

El Gato's men quickly tied them. The horses were brought, and the women were tossed on, belly-down. With another bandit leading Marabell, they filed into the forest.

Thrack motioned for Fester to join the procession. Fester glanced back often in the vain hope that Tukaduka warriors were after them, but none appeared.

El Gato didn't stop until sunset. He chose a clearing high on a switchback where it would be hard for pursuers to get at them. Two bandits were posted as sentries while another attended to the fire.

They hadn't had anything to eat all day, and El Gato sent a couple of men off to find something for their supper.

Fester figured he was safe enough for the time being. The bandits would be busy with the females.

Then El Gato pointed at him and said grimly, "Come over here, my little chicken. I am in the mood for some fun."

CHAPTER THIRTY-ONE

The Tukadukas were busy preparing a great feast.

Some liked their grasshoppers impaled on a stick and roasted over a fire. Others were fond of grasshopper soup. Still others used rocks to pound the hoppers into a pulped paste, and ate them that way.

Not much attention was paid to Nate as he made his way among them to where Pine Cone, Yellow Badger and Chirping Sparrow were seated.

Nate was through being nice. He walked up, cradled his rifle, and bluntly demanded, "I want the coup stick."

"Tonight we will talk," Yellow Badger said.

"I want it now."

"Tonight is better," Chirping Sparrow said.

"Now."

Pine Cone said, "You seem angry, friend."

"With good cause," Nate said. "Every minute I spend here is another minute my wife is in danger."

"We are sorry for her and for you," Pine Cone said.

Nate held out his hand. "The coup stick."

"If only we had more time," Chirping Sparrow said.

"We have never had a problem like this," Yellow Badger remarked.

"There's no problem so long as you hand over the

coup stick." In his frustration, Nat almost added in English, 'Damn it'.

The old men looked at one another and Pine Cone sighed and indicated the ground in front of them.

"Sit with us, friend, and we will talk."

"I don't want to talk. I want the coup stick."

"Please," Pine Cone requested. "Listen to our words so you will understand."

Reluctantly, Nate sat cross-legged with the Hawken across his lap. "Make it short. I want to go to her."

"We understand. We would feel as you do if she was our woman." Pine Cone paused. "Our people are not warriors. We do not like to fight. We like to live in peace with everyone."

"I know that," Nate said testily.

Unperturbed, Pine Cone went calmly on. "We have always been this way. Other tribes think only of fighting and killing. They think only of counting coup. The more enemies their warriors kill, the higher they are regarded."

"I know that, too."

"We do not like violence, Grizzly Killer. We only fight when we must. When the Bloods or others come to our land to harm us, we hide. We would have hidden from Spotted Wolf except he was hurt. We tried to help him."

"That was kind of you," Nate said, wondering where in blazes their leader was going with this.

"When he died we were sorry for him. We put him under the earth so the animals would not eat him and then we divided up his possessions. His horse filled our bellies." Pine Cone smiled and rubbed his. "It was a good horse. The meat was thick and juicy. I hope I eat horse again one day."

Nate fidgeted with impatience.

"His weapons were given to our best hunters. The weapons are well made and will last many winters and help fill our bellies as his horse did."

"Pine Cone," Nate said, bending toward him. "Get to the point."

The old Tukaduka sighed. "Spotted Wolf had a long stick with feathers on it. We did not know it was a coup stick. We do not use them. None of our hunters wanted it because it was not made for throwing. And it would not have made a good stick for digging, either."

"The coup stick," Nate said angrily. "Now." He was about ready to grab the chief and shake him until his teeth rattled.

Pine Cone let out another sigh and offered a feeble smile. "We do not have it."

"What?"

"Since no one wanted it we gave it to our children to play with."

"What?"

"They broke it."

Nate almost said 'what' again. He was so flabbergasted, he felt numb.

"Some of the boys took it into the woods. They saw a snake go under a log and stuck the stick under the log to try and force the snake out so they could catch it and skin it. But the stick broke so they left it there."

"All this time," Nate said.

"That is why we did not give the coup stick to the Bloods when they came for it."

"We were afraid to tell them we broke it for fear they would be mad at us," Yellow Badger said.

"So we ran and hid," Chirping Sparrow threw in.

Nate pounded the ground with a fist. "All this time I've been here and you didn't tell me until now?"

"We didn't want you mad at us," Pine Cone said.

"We have been talking over how best to tell you," Yellow Badger told him.

"Now you know," Chirping Sparrow said.

"God in heaven," Nate said in English. It had dawned on him that he couldn't swap the coup stick for Winona.

"What was that?" Pine Cone said.

In Shoshone Nate said, "My wife. The Bloods will not give her to me now."

"Perhaps you could give them something else for her," Pine Cone said.

"I have nothing they want."

"Elk meat, maybe," Chirping Sparrow said. "Everyone likes elk meat. We like it very much. It is almost as good as horse meat."

"They won't want meat of any kind," Nate said, half-dazed as the enormity of his plight sank in.

"How about if you gave them one of your guns?" Yellow Badger suggested. "Tribes that like to kill always like guns."

"All they will take for her is Spotted Wolf's coup stick."

"All this bother over a stick," Pine Cone said.

"If we knew how, we would make another just like it and you could give them that," Yellow Badger said.

"What will you do?" Chirping Sparrow asked.

"Save her any way I can," Nate said.

"Even if you must take a life?"

"Even if I have to kill every last one of them."

CHAPTER THIRTY-TWO

Winona's punishment was to be gagged as well as retied. Sacripant wasn't gentle about it. All day she lay on the ground, the rope digging painfully into her flesh, the strip of buckskin he had jammed into her mouth making her want to gag. She lay as still as she could, the scent of the earth and the grass in her nostrils, her eyes hooded against the harsh glare of the sun.

The only good thing was that Sacripant and the Bloods left her alone. Some went hunting. Others took their mounts to a nearby stream.

One or another of them, though, always stood guard over her.

Winona hadn't seen sign of Bright Rainbow all day. She was considerably surprised when, without any hint that the girl was there, tiny fingers touched her arm.

The guard had his back to her and was idly gazing into the distance.

Winona glanced over her shoulder.

Bright Rainbow was flat on her belly. She smiled and held up a jagged piece of quartz.

Winona checked on the Blood and felt pressure on the rope around her wrists. She was both elated and worried. All the warrior had to do was turn his head and Bright Rainbow was as good as caught. Her mouth went dry from apprehension. She wanted to wag her head to motion for Bright Rainbow to sneak away but movement might draw the man's attention.

Winona couldn't believe that Bright Rainbow had come out in broad daylight. What was the girl thinking? she asked herself. The only possible answer brought a lump to her throat. If she could have, she would have swept Bright Rainbow into her arms and crushed her to her bosom.

The rope slackened a little.

Winona saw the guard start to turn, and went stiff with dread. He looked at her but showed no emotion other than boredom and turned back again. Twisting her neck, she saw that Bright Rainbow was crouched low behind her.

Bright Rainbow smiled and went on cutting.

Winona kept underestimating how clever the girl was. She felt a scraping sensation and her wrists were free. She quelled an impulse to rub them.

Bright Rainbow twisted to reach the rope around her ankles.

Winona focused on the guard. It was a shame the others had taken his horse to drink, too, as well as her mare.

Bright Rainbow was at it a long while.

A pair of ravens winged overhead. A yellow butterfly flitted erratically about. To the west a hawk and its mate soared in circles.

The rope fell from Winona's legs. She smiled to herself and tested her limbs by moving them slightly. She looked at Bright Rainbow and let her eyes convey her gratitude. The girl beamed. Winona held her hand out and for a moment Bright Rainbow didn't seem to know what she wanted. Then Bright Rainbow gave her the sharp quartz.

Winona rose into a crouch. Once she was up, she didn't waste any time. She crept to the warrior, prepared to slash his throat with the quartz, but the hilt of his knife, jutting from a sheath on his hip, gave her a better idea. As quick as thought, she grabbed it and jerked it out. Once, twice, three times, she buried the long blade in his back.

The Blood arched and gasped. At the third thrust his body sagged. He exhaled a long breath, and collapsed.

Winona glanced about her. The rest of the Bloods could return any time. Her own knife and Hawken and pistols were in a pile, and she hurriedly reclaimed them, along with her powder horn and ammo pouch.

Bright Rainbow had risen and was staring at the dead warrior.

It occurred to Winona that the girl had seen little violence in her life. "I had to do it."

"I understand."

Winona went to her and hugged her. "That was very brave of you."

"I couldn't let them hurt you."

"You took a great risk," Winona said tenderly. "Thank you, little one."

"What do we do now?"

"We stay alive." Winona took her hand and was about to go around the fire when she almost stepped on some roast venison that had been left impaled on a stick. She snatched it up. "When did you eat last?"

"With Nate and you," Bright Rainbow said.

Winona gave her the stick. "Wait until we are safe."
They ran.

Winona's ankles hurt terribly and her wrists were sore but she didn't care. She was free and alive and determined to stay that way.

By the time they reached the woods, they were winded. Winona plunged into the vegetation and went the distance of an arrow's flight before she stopped and squatted. "You can eat now if you want."

Like a ravenous wolf, Bright Rainbow tore into the venison. She chewed with relish, grinning the while, her cheeks bulging. "I was afraid for you."

"And I for you," Winona confessed.

"They will come after us, won't they?"

"Yes."

"We should hide our tracks."

Winona smiled. "The only way to do that is to walk on air."

"We need to find rocky ground. Then we won't leave footprints."

"No wonder you survived on your own for so long. You are very bright."

"I am Tukaduka. We learn to avoid others as soon as we learn to walk. It is so our enemies can't find us."

Winona refrained from mentioning that to the Shoshones and others, the Sheepeaters weren't worth counting coup on. As her cousin Touch The Clouds once put it, killing a Tukaduka was like killing a fawn.

"I am glad Evelyn and you found me," Bright Rainbow said.

Winona fondly touched her cheek.

"It is too bad you can't be my mother."

To that, Winona made no response. Taking the girl's hand, she made off into the timber. Her stomach growled but she didn't ask to share the meat.

Bright Rainbow finished and threw the stick aside. Wiping her mouth with the back of her hand, she asked, "Where are we going?"

"To find my husband."

"What if the Bloods catch up to us before we find him?"

"I won't let them take me again."

"You'll fight them?"

"With my dying breath," Winona said.

CHAPTER THIRTY-THREE

Fester figured his time had come. He went over to El Gato, who had a hand on the hilt of his knife, and gruffly snapped, "What do you want now, you damned lunatic?"

The bandit leader grinned at the three Tukaduka women, who cowered in fear, their eyes averted. "What do you think of our hens?"

"I think you should have your way with them."

El Gato blinked in surprise. "You do?"

Fester nodded. "And if they scream their heads off and bawl and blubber, so much the better."

"Why, little chicken, who would have thought it?" El Gato said, and uttered a cold chuckle. "Or could it be that you want them to make a lot of noise so their men will hear?"

"I never thought of that," Fester lied.

"How *estupido* do you think I am?"El Gato said. "But no matter. We have come far enough that no one will hear their cries. So let us enjoy ourselves. And you, my little chicken, go first."

"How's that again?"

"Don't your ears work? I do you a great honor. You get to have a woman before we do."

"You're joshin'."

"Pick whichever you like. Me, I would choose the

one with the biggest *pechos*, but I have always liked *pechos* more than *piernas* or *nalgas*."

"More than what?"

"I like *tetas*," El Gato said, and motioned. "Go ahead. Enjoy. It is the last *sexo* you will have in this world."

Fester stared at the women.

"What are you waiting for? My men want to take their turns. Don't keep them waiting."

"No," Fester said.

"I honor you with my generosity and you throw it in my face?"

"You call rapin' a female an honor?"

El Gato frowned. "You call it rape. I don't."

"What in hell do you call it, then?"

"I call it doing what a woman would do anyway after a man treats her to a fine meal and flowers and a walk under the stars."

"Most women don't go to bed with a man just because the man brings them daisies."

"That is because their mother says it is bad, or their priest says it is bad. But deep down they want it. Deep down they crave for a man to have their way with them."

"That's the dumbest thing I've ever heard."

"Been with a lot of *putas*, have you?" El Gato scornfully asked.

"What's that?"

"Whores."

"No wonder you think the way you do," Fester said. "Most ladies like to be courted. They like to be married before they lift their skirts. Comparin' whores to married ladies is like comparin' apples to apple pie."

"All women are whores at heart, gringo."

"You're about the biggest ignoramus who ever breathed if you believe that."

"I truly do, little chicken." El Gato grew unusually serious. "My own *madre* was a whore."

"Your very own ma?"

"*Si*. She went to bed with any man with two *pesos* in his pocket."

"Was that the only way she could make ends meet?" Fester had heard that when some women became desperate, they sold their bodies.

"She did it because she liked it. She liked the *pesos* and she liked the *sexo*."

"And gave you the hare-brained idea that all females are the same."

"All women *are* like her. Go up to the most virtuous woman you know and offer her a million Yankee dollars to go to bed with you and she will do it."

"You have too low an opinion of females."

"And you have too high a one. You are like most *hombres*. You put women on a—-how do you say it?" El Gato's brow furrowed. "Ah, yes. You put them on a pedestal. To you they are angels. You treat them as if they don't have the same needs that men do."

"Needs ain't the same for everybody," Fester said. "I never had much use for that sex business."

"Yours does not work?"

"Say again?"

El Gato pointed below Fester's belt. "You have not been with women because you can't?"

His meaning sank in and Fester's neck and face grew

warm. "Why, you damned idiot, it works perfectly fine, I'll have you know. I just never had much interest in having it work."

"How can you not have an interest in *that*?"

"Not all men are randy goats."

El Gato walked over to the women. He cupped the chin of the nearest and turned her head toward them. She tried to pull away but he cuffed her and she froze. "This one is *mas bonita*. Look at her and tell me you don't want her." He put a hand to her bosom. "Tell me you don't want to fondle these beauties?"

"Don't," Fester said.

"Stupid gringo," El Gato said in disgust. "Blushing like a boy. You should be ashamed." He gripped the chin of the second woman. "This one, then? She is plainer but maybe she is more to your taste."

"I said no."

El Gator drew a pistol. Cocking it, he pressed the muzzle to the woman's neck. She mewed and sought to back away and he struck her. With a cry she doubled over, and he put the muzzle to the back of her head.

"Don't," Fester said.

"Make love to her or I kill her."

"You wouldn't."

"Surely you know me better than that by now?"

"Damn you anyway," Fester said. He saw tears in the woman's eyes. "Where am I supposed to do it? In the woods?"

"Right here," El Gato said.

"Where will you and the rest of your cutthroats be?"

"Right here," El Gato said again.

"You're goin' to watch?"

"And cheer you on," El Gato said, and laughed.

"Not in a million years," Fester said.

El Gato cocked the hammer. "You have until I count to ten. If you have not started to undress, you will wear her brains on your buckskins."

CHAPTER THIRTY-FOUR

Nate was saddling his bay when a woman came running into camp. Gasping for breath and covered with sweat, she passed him on the fly. She went another twenty feet and collapsed. Others rushed to her side.

Nate went on preparing to leave. Something had happened but it was none of his concern. He had Winona to think of. He tied his parfleche on and was about to raise his leg to the stirrup when a little girl screamed.

Against his better judgment, Nate went to see why. He shouldered through the Tukadukas to find the woman on her back, her head cradled in the lap of an older female who looked enough like her to be her mother.

Pine Cone and Chirping Sparrow were there.

So was Squirrel Tail. "That is Spotted Fawn," he said quietly, indicating the woman who had collapsed. "She was picking berries with three friends and got a thorn in her moccasin. She stopped and sat down and took the moccasin off to get the thorn out, and while she was doing that, strange men rushed out of the trees and took the other three captive. She waited until she was sure they were gone, then came for help."

"Were the men Bloods?"

"No. They weren't Indians or whites. She has never

seen men like them. They wore wide hats and were darker than whites but not as dark as we are."

"Wide hats? Does she mean *sombreros?*"

"I do not know what those are."

"Sounds to me like they're Mexicans," Nate guessed, although it was rare for anyone from south of the border to be this far north.

Murmuring rippled among the onlookers until Pine Cone raised his arms for silence.

"Enemies have taken Little Antelope, Blue Egg and Waterfall. Half the men will go find them while the rest stay and protect our loved ones."

A burst of activity broke out.

Nate retraced his steps to the bay. He felt sorry for the three women but he had a calamity of his own to deal with. He reached for the reins, and a hand fell on his arm.

"I would ask a favor of you," Pine Cone said.

"I can't."

"You have a horse."

"I have a wife held captive by the Bloods." Nate shrugged the chief's hand off.

"The men who took our women have horses. They are far away by now."

"Damn it," Nate said in English.

"You can catch up to them and bring us word of where they are."

Nate turned. "You ask a lot of me, old man."

"Yes, I am old," Pine Cone said. "I have lived many winters, and with those winters has come wisdom. The wisdom to tell if a man has a good heart or a bad heart. You, Grizzly Killer, have a good heart. Had I not seen you with my own eyes, I would know it to be true because the Shoshones adopted you and they would not adopt someone with a bad heart."

"You keep forgetting about my wife."

"She will be safe until you bring them the coup stick. Is that not what you told us?"

"I don't trust them to keep their word." Nate was thinking of Sacripant.

"I would not, either. But they gave you ten sleeps, did they not? And only a few have gone by. Surely one more will not make a difference."

"You ask too much."

"Three lives, Grizzly Killer," Pine Cone said. "The lives of three young women. Women who, like you, have good hearts. Are their lives not worth saving, just as your wife's is?"

"You could talk a mink out of its coat," Nate said bitterly.

"Spotted Fawn will show you where they were picking berries. It is not far, she says."

"Pine Cone," Nate said wearily.

"Were there any other way, I would not ask. On foot we can not catch them. We will never see the three women again. Their fathers and mothers will not see them. Their husbands will not see them. Their children will not see them."

Nate realized that a lot of the others had come up and were expectantly waiting.

"Will you or won't you, Grizzly Killer?"

Suppressing an oath, Nate turned and swung onto the bay. "I wouldn't have to do this if your people had horses."

"We can't have them," Pine Cone said.

"What's stopping you? The Shoshones have horses. The Crows have horses. The Utes have them. The Flatheads, the Sioux. Every tribe there is except yours."

"I would like for us to have horses but it is impossible," Pine Cone said.

"Nothing is impossible."

"Horses are, for us."

"Why?"

Pine Cone stared at his people and then at the ground and said sheepishly, "We are afraid of them."

CHAPTER THIRTY-FIVE

Fester Simmons stared at the poor Tukaduka with the pistol to the back of her head and asked in her tongue, "What is your name, young woman?"

Her voice quaking with terror, she replied, "I am called Waterfall."

"I am not one of these men. They are evil. They took me captive as they took you, and covered me with these feathers."

"Is the fat one going to kill me?"

"He wants us to make love."

Waterfall's bewilderment was obvious. "Did I hear you right?"

"The one with the gun wants me to make love to you in front of him and all the others."

El Gato suddenly barked, "Enough. What were you telling her?"

"What you want me to do."

"Ah. Then let us get on with it." El Gato grinned. "*Uno. Dos. Tres,*" he slowly counted.

Fester bowed his head. The feathers were enough humiliation for one lifetime. Now this.

The rest of the bandits had gathered around and were leering and sneering in expectation.

"*Cuatro.* That's four in case you don't know."

Fester gazed at Marabell and his plews.

"*Cinco.*"

Fester looked up at the bright blue of the sky and the few fluffy clouds.

"*Seis.*"

Fester breathed in the piney scent of the mountain air and said, "You don't need to go on."

"What was that, little chicken?"

"I'm not goin' to do it," Fester said. "Go ahead and blow her brains out. The shot will carry for miles and her people are bound to hear, but you shoot her anyway."

El Gato's face twisted with venom. "You think I am afraid of a few savages?"

"I told you before. There are hundreds at their get-togethers. Enough to rub out you and the rest of these vermin." Fester looked him in the eyes. "Go ahead and shoot her, you yellow bastard."

With an inarticulate growl, El Gato was on him. Once, twice, and yet again El Gato swung the heavy flintlock, the thud of the blows loud in the clearing.

Fester was rocked back, his head exploding with pain. The world blinked to black and he was vaguely aware of falling and of more blows. This is it, he thought. His time had come. He wished he had lived a while yet. He liked being alive, liked it a lot. He felt another blow and then there was nothing at all for he knew not how long.

It was the feel of cool air on what Fester liked to call his 'unmentionables' that brought him around. He stayed still, wondering if he was in the hereafter. He'd never thought about it much but it made sense to him that a person's clothes didn't go with them into the afterlife. Then the pain hit him and he knew he wasn't dead.

Fester opened his eyes.

Above him stars sparkled.

His head felt funny, as if his brain was floating in oatmeal. His throat was dry as a desert. He tried to swallow and couldn't. His head hurt too much for him to move it so he swiveled his eyes every which way. He was lying in the clearing. The bandits and the women were gone. He figured El Gato had left him for dead.

"My ma always said I had a hard head," Fester croaked, and smiled. The effort cost him. He blacked out again.

When he came to, he tried to sit up and new hurt flooded through him. Not just his head, but his chest, his left hand, his back. He wondered if El Gato had stomped on him after he was down. He wouldn't put it past the son of a bitch.

Fester gazed at the stars and waited for his strength to return, if it ever would. He might be at death's door. He imagined lying there for hours or days and slowly wasting away. Or, worse, a wild animal would smell the blood and come to fill its belly.

That scared him.

Fester couldn't think of a worse way to die than to be eaten alive. To have a beast's fangs tear into his vitals while he was still breathing—-that would be plumb awful.

In the distance a wolf howled.

Closer, a twig snapped.

An elk, Fester told himself, or a deer. Gritting his teeth, he propped his right hand under him and sat up.

God, but it hurt.

He almost passed out again. When he was sure he wouldn't, he slowly looked around. There were no bodies. The three women, then, were still alive. El Gato had taken them with him.

Fester was thankful for that. He liked the Tukadukas. They were such gentle folk.

He went to slide his left hand under him and nearly cried out. He couldn't move his fingers. Raising his hand in front of his face, he found out why. He'd been stomped on, all right. His hand was broken, several of the fingers splayed, his knuckles the size of walnuts. He wouldn't be using that hand any time soon.

Off in the forest, the vegetation crackled.

Fester pricked his ears. Whatever it was, it was big. He grew alarmed when the crackling grew louder. The thing was coming toward him. As much noise as it was making, he reckoned it could only be one thing; a bear.

Fester tried to scramble toward the trees, and couldn't. He was too weak, and he hurt too much. He collapsed onto his side.

He had never felt so helpless in his life.

The crackling stopped.

Fester held his breath. Maybe the bear would leave him be. Bears were unpredictable critters. Most ran at the sight or smell of a human.

For a long, tense minute the silence held. Suddenly there was loud crashing and a gigantic shape burst into the clearing and loomed above him.

"God," Fester said. Closing his eyes, he braced for the end.

CHAPTER THIRTY-SIX

Winona stayed on the move all day. She stopped to rest more often then she would if she were alone, for Bright Rainbow's sake. The girl never complained once about the pace or the hot sun or the rugged terrain.

Late in the afternoon they stopped on a high ridge dotted with pines and spruce. They'd had to climb for half an hour to reach it and Winona's legs ached. A log provided a seat. She patted it and said, "Rest a while, little one."

Bright Rainbow sat and gazed back the way they had come. "They are after us," she said, and pointed.

Winona had seen them, too; a knot of riders, stick figures, some two miles away. "They are a long way off yet."

"When will we find Nate?"

"I hoped we would have by now," Winona said. The Tukaduka were supposed to be in that area.

"I hope nothing happened to him."

So did Winona. Her mate was as capable as any man alive but the wilderness was rife with dangers that could catch even the most wary off-guard.

"Are you ever sorry you took a white man for a husband?" Bright Rainbow asked.

Winona glanced at her sharply. "What kind of question is that?"

"I heard my mother and father talking once about a Crow woman who was with a white trapper," Bright Rainbow said. "My mother said she could never marry a white man. They are too strange."

"Nate is strange at times," Winona said, and laughed. "All men are. But no, I have never regretted sharing my lodge with him. He listens to me. He treats me with respect. He is a good provider and a caring father. No woman could ask for a better husband."

"My mother felt that way about my father. I miss them so much." Bright Rainbow's chin dipped and she closed her eyes.

"There, there." Winona draped an arm over her shoulders. To take her mind off her parents, she said, "I want to thank you again for risking your life to save me."

"I could not let the Bloods hurt you."

"Many girls your age would have been too scared to try what you did."

"I'm not like I used to be," Bright Rainbow said. "Before my mother and father died, I was scared a lot."

"And now?"

"We all die. Being afraid of something that will happen whether we want it to or not is silly."

"That is a very mature outlook."

They were quiet a while and then Bright Rainbow said, "Besides, I don't much care about the rest anymore."

"The rest of what?"

Bright Rainbow swept an arm at the surrounding mountains. "Any of this. I lost my family. Now I'm going to lose you and Evelyn and Nate. What is there to care for?"

"Oh, little one," Winona said."You are too young to have such dark thoughts."

"I do not feel young," Bright Rainbow said. "I feel very old."

Since they'd first met, Winona had marveled at the girl's calm bearing. It had also puzzled and bothered her. Bright Rainbow lost her parents under gruesome circumstances. She'd seen them torn apart before her very eyes. Yet the child showed little emotion over the loss. It was unnatural.

"Shouldn't we keep going?"

"You don't want to rest a while longer?" Winona asked.

"I do not."

"Very well."

They hiked over the crest. Below stretched a verdant valley split by a blue ribbon.

"Water," Winona said, pointing.

They walked faster.

Winona missed her mare. She kept her fingers crossed, as the the whites liked to say, that they didn't run into anything inclined to eat them. Or gore them. Or trample them.

Winona remembered a time Nate took her to St. Louis. They'd needed to have his Hawken repaired and he always took it to the Hawken brothers. One evening they'd eaten at a restaurant and a couple at the next table struck up a conversation. City people, they'd been mesmerized by Nate's tales of the high country.

At one point the woman had looked at Winona and said, "I don't see how you do it, my dear. Live in the wilds, I mean. I certainly couldn't."

"You get used to it," Winona had said.

"Get used to grizzlies that can rip you apart? Get used to having rattlesnakes underfoot? To hostiles always out to lift your hair?" The woman had shuddered. "I would live in constant dread."

Winona supposed a lot of whites saw it that way. But the dangers were only part of wilderness life, and a small part, at that. Whole weeks and months and sometimes even years went by in perfect peace. Incidents like this were exceptions, not the norm.

Maybe it was her nature but Winona didn't belabor the bad things in life. She concentrated on the good things. In her family and in their home. To her, each day was a feast of opportunity. Life wasn't to be dreaded because of what *might* happen but savored for what did.

"Winona?" Bright Rainbow said.

"Yes, little one?"

"Are you afraid of bears?"

"A little," Winona admitted.

"Which are you afraid of the most? Black bears or the big brown bears? The grizzlies?"

"I would rather run into a black bear than a grizzly any day. Black bears almost always run away. Grizzlies sometimes do and sometimes don't, and they are a lot harder to kill than black bears." Winona smiled. "Why do you ask?"

Bright Rainbow pointed at a stand of aspens up ahead. "Because a grizzly is staring at us."

CHAPTER THIRTY-SEVEN

"I'm not the Almighty," Nate King said. Swinging down from the bay, he sank to a knee. "Who are you, old-timer? How are you involved with the women-stealers?"

Fester wanted to pinch himself. The gigantic shape he'd taken for a bear was a horse and its rider. He was so overcome with joy that he had to try twice to speak. "Fester Simmons is my handle. I was stole by the same bunch as stole those Tukaduka gals. They made me their chicken and then left me for dead."

Nate was amazed to discover that the old man was, in fact, partly covered with feathers. "Their chicken?"

"It was El Gato's idea of a joke. He's the leader of the bandits."

Nate bent closer. The pale starlight revealed a welt on Simmons' temple and dark bruises where the feathers didn't cover his skin. "They beat you?"

"El Gato again," Fester said, grimacing. "He stomped me into the ground. My hand is busted. Might be a rib or two is cracked, as well."

"Are the women still alive?"

"Last I saw. But I can't say for how long. El Gato's outfit is snake mean."

"I'll sit you up," Nate offered, and went to slide his

hand under the old man's back.

"I'd be more obliged for britches," Fester said. "I don't much like lyin' here in the altogether."

"I don't have any that would fit you." Nate was twice the man's size, if not more. "They'd be so baggy, they'd keep falling down."

"Baggy is all right if you've got some rope."

Nate had been about to stop for the night so he wasn't bothered by this latest delay. It had gotten too dark to read sign anyway. Opening his parfleche, he took out his spare pants and a coil of rope he always had handy.

Fester's broken hand was hurting so bad, it was all he could do not to cry out. He felt weak and vulnerable and hated being bare-assed naked. "Say," he said when the big man came back, "you haven't told me who you are."

Nate introduced himself.

"King?" Fester said. "King, you say?" The name jarred a recollection. "Weren't you a trapper years back?"

"I was," Nate went to hand him the britches and realized that with his broken hand, the old man couldn't pull them on.

"Did you ever go to the rendezvous?"

"Every year," Nate said. Each summer, trappers from all over the Rockies had gathered on the Green River or some other site to sell their plews, drink, swap tall tales, and generally have a rowdy time.

"I bet I saw you there," Fester said. He had been to all of them, too.

Nate laid the pants flat on the ground. "Stick your

feet in these and I'll hitch them up for you."

"I can do it my own self, thank you very much." Fester would be damned if he'd let another man dress him. Using his right hand, he got his feet into the pants and then pulled and yanked until they were past his knees. He couldn't tug them any higher unless he lifted his bottom and he was still too weak to do that.

"Here," Nate said. Moving around behind him, he slipped his hands under Fester's arms and raised him up. "Try it now."

Fester quickly got the pants up to his waist. "I'm obliged."

Nate set him down, picked up the rope, and proceeded to cut a suitable length.

"I miss the days when beaver fur was in its prime," Fester mentioned. "I was earnin' a thousand dollars or more a year. These days, I'm lucky if my plews bring in two hundred."

"You still trap for a living?" Nate asked in mild surprise. All the trappers he knew had long since moved on to other means of making a living.

"Why not?" Fester said. "My needs are few. And I love trappin'. Love it more than anything. And not just beaver. I trap all kinds of animals, from coons to bears. Last year a white mink fetched me pretty near four dollars down to Bent's."

"That's a good price," Nate said. But then, white fur was rare and always brought top dollar. It told him a lot that the old man had stuck with trapping long after most had quit.

"I have me some nice ones in this year's haul," Fester said, "but that bastard El Gato has them. If it's the last thing I do, I'll get them back, and my mule, Marabell, too."

Before Nate quite realized what he was saying, he said, "We'll get them back together."

"You'd help an old cuss like me?"

"So long as we do it quick," Nate said, and went on to explain, briefly, about Winona and the Bloods.

Fester listened with keen interest. "Well now," he said when Nate finished, "it seems to me your missus is more important than my plews. I'll go on alone. You light out after her."

A great fondness came over Nate. "That's damned decent of you. But you're forgetting the three Tukaduka women."

"What are they to you?"

"Human beings."

"Are they worth losin' your wife over?"

Nate didn't answer.

"I didn't think so," Fester said.

"We'll get some sleep and head out at first light," Nate proposed.

"I have a better idea. They couldn't have gotten that far. If we head right out, we'll catch up to them long before mornin'."

"It's slow going, tracking at night," Nate said, "and they'd see our torch."

"Could be we don't need one," Fester said. "I know those lunkheads. They keep a fire goin' all night. We're bound to spot it."

Nate liked the idea. The sooner he was done with this mess, the sooner he could fly to Winona. "First I'll rig a splint for that hand of yours. Come sunrise, you'll have your plews and your mule back, both."

"Or be dead," Fester said.

CHAPTER THIRTY-EIGHT

Winona looked up and jammed her Hawken to her shoulder but she didn't shoot. The bear that was staring at them wasn't a grizzly. It was brown like grizzlies were but it didn't have the telltale hump.

Black bears weren't always black. Sometimes they were a cinnamon hue, or brown like this one. It was also young, not more than a year or so old.

"It's only a black bear," Winona said in relief. Raising her rifle over her head, she shook it and hollered and the bear wheeled and hastened off into the timber.

Bright Rainbow laughed. "You scared him off!"

"If it had been a grizzly it might have been different."

They hiked on. After a while Bright Rainbow looked back and said, "The Bloods are closer."

"They have horses."

"Do you think they will catch up to us before the sun goes down?"

"Let's hope they don't," Winona answered. She held to a fast walk and Bright Rainbow never once complained.

Sacripant and company were still half a mile away when the sun dipped below the horizon.

"We're safe until morning," Winona said. She kept on until she noticed Bright Rainbow was having trouble keeping up. At the next clearing they came to, she stopped and announced, "We'll rest here until daybreak."

"I can keep going."

Winona touched the girl's cheek. "I admire you more than you can know."

"For what?"

"I want you to lie down and make yourself as comfortable as you can."

Bright Rainbow didn't argue. Hardly had she curled on her side than she was out to the world.

Winona tried to get some sleep but it proved difficult. It didn't help that the mountains echoed to the howls of wolves and the occasional roar of a bear, or that coyotes were in constant chorus. She dozed off a few times and was always startled awake.

The sun hadn't yet risen but the sky had lightened to a shade of gray when they were under way.

Dawn broke, casting the Rockies in a golden glow. They were high up in tall pines, the kind Winona's people and others used as lodge poles. A carpet of needles was underfoot and their footfalls made no sound.

"It's so quiet," Bright Rainbow whispered.

Winona had noticed the same thing. It was almost *too* quiet. There should be birds singing and squirrels chattering but there was only an ominous stillness. She didn't like it. "We need to find something to eat to keep our strength up. If we—-." Winona abruptly stopped and tilted her head. "Did you hear something?"

"Yes," Bright Rainbow said. "It sounded like a horse."

Putting a finger to her lips, Winona cautiously moved forward. Almost immediately she spotted a dark mass partially hidden by the trees. As she watched, part of it moved. The horse's tail, she realized, swishing back and forth. She crouched and motioned for Bright Rainbow to do the same.

"Who can it be?"

Winona thought she knew. Some of the Bloods, by pushing their mounts hard, had circled ahead and were waiting in ambush. It was clever of them. But she could be clever too. She crabbed to the right and once the horse was out of sight, rose and jogged in a wide loop that brought them out of the lodgepoles well past the horse and whoever was on it.

Before them spread open ground broken by islands of trees and crisscrossed by washes. A perfect place for them to lose themselves.

"You never answered me," Bright Rainbow said.

"I suspect it was the Bloods."

"But you outsmarted them."

"We were lucky. If that horse hadn't whinnied, we would have walked right into an ambush."

"You're the smartest person I've ever met," Bright Rainbow said. "You're smarter than my mother and I always thought no one was smarter than her."

"You give me too much credit," Winona said.

"Nate says you're smarter than he is," Bright Rainbow imparted. "He says you're the smartest in the whole world."

"He said that? You must forgive him. He is overly fond of me."

"You speak more tongues than anybody, he says."

"I speak five or six fairly well. There are people who speak more."

"Nate says you are so smart, it scares him sometimes. What does he mean by that?"

"He is male. Men say silly things. When you are older and you are living with a man of your own, you will understand."

"I don't want a man of my own. I don't think I will ever be a wife."

"I didn't think so, either, at your age."

"What changed your mind?"

"I grew up," Winona said. Suddenly she halted and pivoted on her heel.

Back in the woods hoofs thudded. Horses were rapidly approaching.

"Quick," Winona said. She sprinted into a dry wash. Pebbles clattered from under her moccasins as she flattened and raised her head high enough to see over.

They'd made it just in time.

Out of the trees trotted three riders. In the lead was Sacripant. Behind him were Three Bulls and another warrior. They drew rein and conversed in low tones. Sacripant pointed to the west. Three Bulls pointed back the way they came.

"What are they talking about?" Bright Rainbow whispered.

"Whether we are in front of them or in back of them," was Winona's guess.

"Can you shoot them from here?"

Winona hadn't even considered that. They were within range, though. She was confident she could drop one but the other two would be on her before she could reload. "It would be unwise."

"Shoot Three Bulls. He's the one who wants the coup stick. Without him they have no reason to be here. The rest will go home."

"That might not be wise either," Winona said. Should she and the girl fall into the Bloods' clutches, they would surely suffer.

Just then the argument ended and Sacripant, Three Bulls and the third warrior gigged their mounts toward the wash.

CHAPTER THIRTY-NINE

It took longer than Nate expected. Daybreak was less than an hour off when an orange glow danced in the darkness ahead. Drawing rein, he said, "You were right. They're careless."

Fester had one hand on Nate's shoulder and his hurt hand pressed to his side. The pain wouldn't relent. His hand was so busted up, he figured it would be six months or better before he could use it again, if then. "They're dumb, is what they are."

Nate poked the bay with his heels. "When we stop, you stay with my horse."

"Like hell. I may be old but I can do my part."

"I wasn't thinking of your age," Nate said. "I was thinking of your hand."

"Lend me a pistol and I'll make do. I don't need two hands to shoot."

"It will take you forever to reload using just one."

"I've had to do it one-handed before," Fester said. "The time I busted my wrist, and another time when I burned my fingers."

"I'll think about it."

"There are too many for you to handle by your lonsesome," Fester argued. Plus, he wanted to be the one to shoot El Gato. He owed that bastard.

"I don't aim to go up against them alone," Nate set

him straight. "I figure to sneak in, get the women, and sneak out again."

"They always have someone on guard," Fester warned him. "And these are killers we're talkin' about. One shout, and they'll come out from under their blankets shootin'."

The fire was farther than it seemed.

They descended a steep wooded slope to a stream, crossed over, and climbed an even steeper slope on the other side. When they were a couple of hundred yards below the flickering finger, Nate drew rein.

"This is as far as you go."

"Damn you," Fester said.

Nate helped him down, and dismounted. He tied the reins to a limb and turned to go.

"At least leave me a pistol to defend myself with," Fester requested, holding out his good hand."

"You promise to stay with the bay?"

"My solemn word."

Nate slid a flintlock from under his belt. "Don't shoot me or the women. We'll be coming fast."

"What do you take me for? A simpleton?"

Nate went on alone. The slope was so steep he had to bend forward to keep from losing his balance. He was mildly taken aback to find that there were two men who were awake, not just one. They were sitting across the fire from one another and sipping coffee.

The last twenty yards, Nate crawled. From behind a log he counted the sleepers and surveyed the camp.

The bandits had made other mistakes besides kindling their fire where it could be seen. Their horses and Fester's mule were too near the trees, tied to a rope stretched between saplings, instead of hobbled. The bandits were sleeping too far from the string. And their captives weren't next to the fire where they could be easily watched but were a good ten feet from it.

Fester's descriptions enabled Nate to tell which one was El Gato. The bandit leader was on his back, his big belly rising and falling. Near him was the one bandit who wasn't Mexican and wasn't wearing a sombrero. Mortan Thrack, according to Fester, was the quickest and the deadliest.

The Tukaduka women appeared to be asleep.

Nate crawled in a circle that brought him close to the horses and Marabell. All were dozing save a sorrel that pricked its ears. Praying the animal wouldn't give him away, Nate went around them.

At the fire the two bandits were talking in hushed, bitter tones. They weren't happy about something and kept glancing at El Gato.

Nate crawled to the captives, careful to keep them between him and the fire. He lightly touched a bare shoulder. The young woman's eyes snapped open and for an instant he thought she would scream. "I am a friend," he quickly whispered into her ear in the Shoshone tongue. "Pine Cone asked me to help you."

The mention of the chief's name had a calming effect. She glanced at the two bandits by the fire and rolled over so she faced him. "I am Waterfall."

Nate drew his bowie and cut her free. "Wake the others but do it quietly." He figured they were less likely to cry out if she did it. "Then I'll cut their ropes."

A bandit at the fire yawned and stretched. The other one refilled his tin cup.

Waterfall shook the woman next to her and whispered in her ear. The second woman then quietly woke the third. Both fixed wondering gazes on Nate.

"I don't suppose any of you can ride a horse?" Nate whispered as he cut.

"None of us ever have," Waterfall said.

Nate frowned. Escaping on horseback would be easier than escaping on foot. He slashed the last of the ropes and slid the bowie into its sheath. "I want all of you to lie still. I'm going to spook their horses. They will run after them and we will slip away. Don't move until I say to."

"We will do exactly as you wish," Waterfall assured him.

Nate made for the string. His back was to the fire and he twisted so he could keep an eye on the two men. When one looked toward the women, he froze. The man said something that caused the other to smirk. The first man cupped himself and the other laughed. Nate could imagine what they were talking about.

Reaching the horses, Nate eased onto his side and reached down to grip the bowie. A slash or two and the deed would be done.

That was when the man called Morton Thrack sat up.

CHAPTER FORTY

Winona didn't like to kill. She had before, and often relived the killings in dreams so vivid, they jarred her awake. She understood that there were times when it had to be done but she would rather not take a life if she could help it. She knew her husband felt the same.

Their son wasn't like them. Zach could kill without hesitation and had told them that it never bothered him afterward. How he could be that way, when they had raised him with so much love, and when they had tried to instill in him consideration for others, was a mystery.

Nate believed that the Shoshone practice of counting coup was to blame. It was true that Shoshone males earned renown and respect through valor in combat. But her people weren't bloodthirsty. They didn't live 'just' for the war path, like some tribes.

Neither, certainly, did Shoshone women. They were devoted to the welfare of their loved ones and the upkeep of their lodge. It was rare for a Shoshone woman to take a life.

So now, as her three enemies came toward the wash in which she was hidden, even though she knew she should shoot them, Winona hesitated.

"What are you waiting for?" Bright Rainbow whispered.

Throwing the Hawken's stock to her shoulder,

Winona was about to take aim when Sacripant drew rein. His companions stopped too.

Sacripant shifted in the saddle and looked back and said something in the Blood Tongue. Three Bulls answered. To Winona's relief, they reined around and rode to the forest. At the tree line they dismounted.

"What are they doing?" Bright Rainbow wondered.

"Waiting for the others," was Winona's guess.

"Can you shoot them from here?"

"They are out of range."

"Too bad."

"Yes, isn't it." Winona slid down to the bottom of the wash. "Follow me."

They wound along until they came to a bend in the shadow of a stand of spruce. Scrambling up the side, they crawled into the trees and moved to where she could see their pursuers. The horses were there—-but Sacripant and Three Bulls and the other warrior weren't.

Winona forgot herself and blurted in English, "What in the world?"

"Where are they?" Bright Rainbow asked.

"Maybe in the woods."

"Why did they leave their horses?"

"I don't know," Winona admitted. It troubled her. She recalled how Sacripant had stopped so suddenly and turned away from the wash and said a few words to the others. Her intuition flared, and she shoved the Hawken at Bright Rainbow. "Hold this for me. I need to climb a tree."

"What for?"

"I think Sacripant might have seen the sun gleam off

my rifle."

"It's heavy," Bright Rainbow said. She held the Hawken at arm's length as if afraid it would bite her.

Winona stepped to a spruce. The branches were so thick, she had to climb halfway up before she could see back along the wash.

Dread rippled through her and she descended so fast, she slipped and nearly fell. Dropping from the bottom limb, she grabbed the Hawken in one hand and Bright Rainbow's wrist in the other.

"What's wrong?"

"We must run for our lives."

"They're after us?"

"Yes."

Winona was upset with herself for not catching on sooner. Nate had always warned her about barrel shine, as he called it.

She also regretted not killing Sacripant when she had the chance. Her soft-heartedness could cost them.

"Will they take us captive or try to kill us?" Bright Rainbow asked.

"Does it matter?" It didn't to Winona. She wouldn't let them take her alive. "Can you run any faster, little one?"

"I am going as fast as I can."

Winona hid her worry. When an isolated boulder loomed, she ducked around to the other side. Squatting with her back to it, she said, "Take a minute to catch your breath."

"I'm fine," Bright Rainbow panted.

Open grass stretched before them. The boulder was the last cover for quite a ways.

Winona half-expected Sacripant's mocking shout.

"You can hear me, yes, *belle femme?* You have given us a good chase but it is over."

Winona didn't respond.

"Come now, *ma cherie.* We know where you are. Do not be childish."

"I hear you," Winona hollered.

"*Bon.* Drop your weapons and step out with your hands where we can see them. The *petite*, too."

"As my husband would say, no can do."

"Be reasonable, Winona," Sacripant said. "You can't get away. Surrender, for the girl's sake if not for your own. I will give you a few minutes to think it over."

Winona didn't need that long. "You want us, come and get us."

CHAPTER FORTY-ONE

Nate King didn't move a muscle as Thrack cast off his blanket and rose. Instead of going to the fire, Thrack stared at the women and then gazed about the clearing as if he suspected something was amiss.

Nate lay in a patch of deep darkness and Thrack didn't see him. He wouldn't be in darkness long, though. To the east a glimmer of impending dawn lit the vault of sky. He was running out of time.

Morton Thrack put his hands on two of his pistols and walked to the fire. He addressed the two men in Spanish and one shook his head and the other said something.

Nate drew his bowie. Holding it low so the firelight wouldn't gleam on the blade, he severed the picket rope. The line sagged but the horses didn't react.

Morton Thrack moved over near the women.

Nate hoped the Tukadukas had the presence of mind not to move or reveal they were awake. Then he remembered. He'd left the cut ropes lying beside them. If Thrack looked down, he'd see them.

After an eternity. Thrack turned back to the fire and hunkered.

Nate snaked around the horses. Straightening, he let out with his best imitation of a bear's roar and smacked several of the animals on the rump.

The horses exploded into motion, stampeding straight at the fire.

Morton Thrack and the two Mexicans leaped to their feet. They had no time to run before the horses were on them. A horse slammed into a bandit and he went down. The other was sent stumbling.

Morton Thrack, though, with incredible agility, avoided a horse bearing down on him.

The next moment the animals were across the clearing and into the woods.

Nate bounded into the undergrowth before anyone could spot him.

Yells erupted. The sleeping bandits came out from under their blankets clutching pistols and rifles and glancing every which way in bewilderment.

El Gato bellowed and all but two of the bandits ran after the horses.

The two were El Gato, himself, and Morton Thrack.

Nate had counted on all of them going. He raised his Hawken. El Gato and Thrack had their backs to him and it went against his nature to shoot someone from behind but it had to be done. Movement stayed his trigger finger.

The three women were getting to their feet. Like sheep trying to slip away from a pair of wolves, they backed toward the forest. They were looking around as if unsure which way they should go.

Nate moved into the open and beckoned.

Waterfall saw him and pulled the others in his direction.

Intent on the women, Nate almost didn't notice when El Gato turned. The bandit leader saw the Tukadukas. For several heartbeats El Gato was rooted in surprise. Then he shouted and extended a pistol.

Nate shot him. He rushed his aim and the slug caught El Gato high in the shoulder.

Even as the Hawken boomed, Morton Thrack whirled. His hands filled with flintlocks and he cocked them and snapped off a shot.

Lead buzzed Nate's ear. "Hurry!" he shouted to the women, and swooped his right hand to a pistol. The females reached him and he practically shoved them into the trees. He followed, and the woods closed around them.

Puzzled as to why Thrack had only fired the one time, Nate looked back.

Thrack was helping El Gato to stand.

"Run," Nate urged the women. As they went he hastily explained that Fester Simmons and his horse weren't far away and they must get there quickly.

"The old man is still alive?" Waterfall said. "Good. He was nice. He tried to help us."

They went as fast as they dared. It was too dark to run flat-out.

Nate kept expecting Morton Thrack to come after them but they descended without incident. "We're almost there."

"Blue Egg and Little Antelope and I thank you for what you have done," Waterfall said.

"We're not safe yet," Nate cautioned. They had miles to cover before they reached the rescue party, and the bandits were bound to pursue them. He rounded a pine and there was the bay, all by itself.

Nate drew up short.

"Where is the old man?" Waterfall asked.

Nate had a terrible hunch that he knew. "Stay here," he said, and whirled.

He prayed he wasn't too late.

CHAPTER FORTY-TWO

Fester waited until Nate King vanished into the night to climb after him. It was hard going. His body hurt all over. His hand was worse. Once he bumped it against a tree and had to grit his teeth to keep from screaming.

It angered Fester that Nate had asked him to stay put. He'd endured indignity on top of indignity. He'd suffered a severe beating. He'd had his mule and his furs taken. "Stay put, my ass," he grumbled.

El Gato didn't know it yet, but there would be a reckoning.

Fester was winded and tired when he reached the clearing. He stopped shy of the ring of firelight and smiled on seeing Marabell and his plews. He also saw Nate, sneaking toward the women.

Fester fingered the flintlock Nate had given him. He was tempted—-God, was he tempted—-to put a ball into El Gato's snoring bulk. But he elected to wait. Crouching behind an oak, he marveled at how silently Nate went about cutting the Tukadukas free. When Nate moved to the horse string, Fester circled to be near Marabell. He had a hunch what Nate was going to do and gave a low whistle that only the keen ears of a horse—-or a mule—-would hear.

Marabell swung her head toward him.

"That's my girl," Fester whispered. "It's me, all right. You come to me, you hear?"

Nate King moved behind the animals and uttered the loudest roar Fester ever heard human vocal chords make. The horses bolted. So did Marabell. But instead of running toward the other side of the clearing, as the horses were doing, she wheeled and crashed into the woods and came right to him.

"God, I've missed you, you ornery cuss," Fester said affectionately. He wanted to hug her but he hurriedly led her further away. He heard shots and yells and curses and then shots. When he had gone far enough, he tied Marabell to a tree, patted her neck, and went back as fast as his battered body allowed.

Nate and the Tukadukas were gone. So were all the bandits except for Thrack and the man Fester hated most in the world.

El Gato had been shot. He was seated by the fire, a hand to his shoulder, blood trickling from between his fingers. He looked more mad than hurt.

Morton Thrack was bent over him.

El Gato growled a few words, and Thrack hurried in the direction the horses had gone.

Fester grinned. For once things were going his way. He crept into the open and was only a few feet from El Gato when El Gato looked up.

"You!"

"Happy to see me?" Fester pointed the flintlock at the bastard's face. "Did you miss your little chicken?"

El Gato started to lower his hand to the pistols at his waist.

"Go ahead," Fester said. "I'm itchin' to blow your

brains out."

"You won't shoot me," El Gato said, but he put his hand back over his wound.

"This should be good," Fester said. "Give me a reason why you think I won't."

"Because if you do my men will come."

Fester's grin widened. "I'm plumb scared."

"What you are is *stupide*. You should be far away by now."

"You're the one who's dumb." Fester felt a thrill at what he was about to do. "Toss your pistols," he said.

El Gato scowled but he carefully plucked both from under his belt and threw them to one side.

"Now the knife."

"I should have killed you when I had the chance."

Fester grinned when the blade thunked down. "There now. We can get to it."

El Gato wet his thick lips. "To what, old man?"

"There are some things in this world a man can't abide and still call himself a man," Fester said, moving so he stood next to the pistols El Gato had dropped. "Being put upon. Being treated like pond scum. Being beat. Being stripped half-naked and tarred with feathers."

El Gato smirked. "Yet I did all of those things to you."

"Yes, you did," Fester said, and shot him in the left knee.

Howling in agony, El Gato fell onto his side and clutched his leg and rolled back and forth.

Fester let go of Nate King's pistol and snatched one of those El Gato had dropped. He cocked the piece and when El Gato stopped thrashing and lay gasping for breath, he shot him in the other knee.

El Gato shrieked. He swore. He bucked and writhed.

Fester picked up the other loaded pistol. He waited for the bandit leader to stop thrashing to grin and say, "Havin' fun?"

"I curse you, gringo," El Gato spat. "I curse your mother. She was a *puta*. I curse your father. He was a *bastardo*. What do you say to that?"

"I say good riddance." Fester took aim.

Just then a figure in a black hat and vest raced into the clearing holding a pair of pistols pointed at him.

Twin thunderclaps shattered the morning.

CHAPTER FORTY-THREE

Winona remembered Nate saying that there were times in life when a person had to draw a line in the sand. She had drawn hers. She was tired of running. She would end it, here. And she must do so before the rest of the Bloods arrived.

"Stay down," she said to Bright Rainbow when the girl started to stand.

Around them the waist-high grass rustled to the breeze.

The boulder was too sheer and smooth for Winona to climb. But at least it protected their backs. She pressed her Hawken to her shoulder, and waited. She figured that when they came it would be in a rush, all three at once.

"If you give me a pistol I can help," Bright Rainbow said. "I've seen Nate and you shoot. I know how to do it."

"No," Winona said without looking away from the grass.

"Why not?"

"You are too young to kill."

"How old do you have to be?"

Winona knew that her cousin, Touch The Clouds, slew his first man when he was eleven. A band of Lakotas had raided their village and Touch The Clouds rushed to its defense along with everyone else. "Don't distract me."

"All I have to do is pull that little stick part at the top and squeeze that other little stick part at the bottom. Is that right?"

"Quiet," Winona whispered. She was straining her ears for the slightest sound.

"I will only shoot when you say."

"Hush," Winona said more sternly. She thought she'd heard something. She turned, and suddenly the grass to her right parted and a warrior sprang. He was on her before she could bring the Hawken to bear. With one hand he grabbed the barrel and shoved it aside while simultaneously clamping his other hand on her throat and slamming her against the boulder. Her head cracked hard. Her vision swam and her legs nearly buckled. His fingers gouged so deep into her neck that she couldn't breathe. She let go of the Hawken and grabbed for a pistol but he seized her wrist. He had her, and they both knew it, and he grinned and tilted back his head to yell to his companions.

Bright Rainbow kicked him. She stood and stepped in close and drove her foot into his knee.

The Blood's face twisted in pain. With a savage snarl, he released Winona's wrist and backhanded Bright Rainbow as she went to kick him again.

Instantly, Winona closed her hand on a pistol. She yanked it out, cocking it as she drew. Jamming the muzzle against his belly, she fired.

The heavy ball cored the Blood's body and burst out his spine. He staggered, his hands over his stomach, and looked at her in astonishment. He turned and staggered toward the grass and pitched onto his face. His legs convulsed a few times and he was still.

Winona snatched up the Hawken. She shoved the spent pistol under her belt and bent to help Bright Rainbow stand.

"We got him, didn't we?" Bright Rainbow said, smiling, heedless of a welt on her cheek.

"Yes," Winona said softly. "We did." She drew her other pistol and held it out. "Don't use this unless you are sure."

"I understand." Bright Rainbow held it as if it were an egg that would break if she clasped it too hard.

"Keep an eye out for me." Winona leaned the Hawken against her leg and set to reloading the spent pistol.

From out of the grass came a shout in the Blood language. A few seconds later it was repeated.

"Your friend is dead, Sacripant," Winona hollered. "The same will happen to you and Three Bulls unless you let us go."

"You have killed Yellow Bear, *femme*? That is very bad for you," came an answering shout from off in the grass.

Winona reached into her ammo pouch for a patch and ball.

"We would have let you live. But not now. Anyone who slays a Kainai must be slain in turn. *Vouz comprenez*?"

Winona tugged to extract the ramrod from its housing under the barrel.

"It is a shame, pretty one," Sacripant called out. "I had plans for you and me. Such nice plans they were."

"You would be dead before you laid a finger on me," Winona replied. She wanted to keep him talking while she reloaded.

"You have a formidable spirit, Winona King. But you are too headstrong. A woman should know her place."

"What place is that?"

"To always do as the man wants. To live to please him. To serve him. I would have taught you this."

"How? By beating it into me?" Winona had noticed that each time he spoke it came from a different spot.

"If that is what it took, oui."

"I will tell you something, Sacripant." Winona was almost done. "My husband has never once hit me. In all our winters together, he has never so much as raised a hand to me. He treats me as his friend as much as his wife. He respects me. I am not his slave."

"How quaint," the *voyageur* replied. "But then, your husband has been infected with white ideas. It has made him less of a man."

Winona bristled at the insult. "My Nate is more of a man than you'll ever be."

"A wife always defends her husband, even when he is weak."

Winona laughed, then shouted, "My husband is many things, but no one has ever accused him of being that."

"It is a pity, really," Sacripant said, and he was closer now. "Such beautiful times you and I could have had, *ma cherie.*"

"I do not sleep with pigs."

There was a long silence and then Sacripant said,

"Prepare to die, bitch."

CHAPTER FORTY-FOUR

Nate raced into the clearing and saw Morton Thrack point two pistols at Fester Simmons. Nate already had his Hawken cocked and pressed to his shoulder, and he aimed and fired at the same instant that Thrack did.

The slug caught Thrack in the temple and jolted him back a step. His eyes rolled up into his head and the killer pitched to his knees and keeled over.

The next moment Fester fired, his pistol shoved virtually in El Gato's face.

El Gato's nose dissolved in a shower of flesh and cartilage. The bandit leader fell back, bucked violently, and let out a long last breath.

Nate ran over. "Are you all right?"

Fester seemed to be in a daze. "You came back for me?"

"Why wouldn't I?" Nate replied as he set to reloading.

The other bandits had heard the shots. From off in the forest came their excited shouts.

Fester picked up the flintlock Nate had lent him. "Here's your pistol."

Nate took it and slid it under his belt. "We're going to have company soon."

"Eh?" Fester said.

Loud crashing proved Nate right.

"There are six of those buzzards left," Fester mentioned.

"Let's get under cover."

Nate headed across the clearing. He realized the old man wasn't following and looked back.

Fester had gone to Thrack and was helping himself to two pistols tucked under Thrack's belt. "These are loaded." Turning, he hurried to Nate, limping a little with each step.

"Are you sure you're all right?"

Instead of answering, Fester ducked behind a small pine.

Nate followed suit.

None too soon. The woods disgorged four of the bandits, who stopped short at the sight of El Gato and Morton Thrack.

"*Madre de dios!*"

"That's Sabino," Fester whispered. "The dark one next to him is called Pedro."

It was Pedro who glanced around the clearing and snapped orders. "*Debemos encontrar a quien hizo esto. Difundir y fuera a buscarlo. No puede haber llegado muy lejos.*"

"Any idea what he was jabberin' about?" Fester asked.

"No." Nate raised his Hawken. "Don't fire until I say to."

"Just so you know," Fester said, "I'm not much of a pistol shot."

The bandits started to spread out and had taken only a few steps when the brush crackled and the last two

204

bandits arrived. On horseback. They drew rein and stared in consternation at El Gato.

"*Puede ser?*" one said.

"*Usted tiene ojos,*" Pedro said. "*Busqueda de su asesino.*"

"*Si,*" the man on horseback replied.

Both riders started across the clearing.

"Take the one on the left," Nate whispered, and sighted down his barrel at the bandit on the right. He waited until the horses were almost on them and said, "Now."

The Hawken and one of Fester's pistols boomed. The bandit on the right rose in the stirrups, clutched at his chest, and toppled. The bandit on the left was hit in the shoulder and lost his grip on his rifle. Frantic not to be shot again, he reined around to get out of there.

Pedro shouted, and he and the rest raised their guns and let loose a volley.

"Down!" Nate cried, flattening as lead chipped at the the tree trunks and branches. Drawing a pistol, he fired at a bandit who was rushing them and the man gave the illusion of diving head-first into the earth.

Fester was taking aim as best he could with only one hand. He shot, and missed.

The wounded bandit on horseback made it to the woods across the clearing. So, too, did Pedro and Sabino and one other.

"There's only four now," Fester said.

Nate commenced to reload, his fingers flying. He loaded his pistol and snatched one of Fester's and set to reloading that.

"We shouldn't stay in one spot," Fester warned.

"I know."

Nate had to reload for both of them. Every nerve prickling, he listened for the bandits but all he heard was the crackling of the fire.

Fester had his broken hand to his side and was staring at El Gato. He smiled and said, "I can die happy knowin' I made maggot bait of that son of bitch."

"Try not to."

"It's funny," Fester said.

"What is?"

"I haven't done much worthwhile in my life. But here I am in the seer of my years and I rub out a worthless gob of spit who killed more folks than I have fingers and toes."

"You did good."

"I did, didn't I?"

The crack of a twig warned Nate to hurry. He shoved the reloaded flintlock at Fester, put a finger to his lips to caution silence, and crouched down.

Fester imitated him, only slower.

Part of a thicket moved even though the wind was still.

Nate centered the Hawken's sights.

Fester started to cough and covered his mouth with his forearm. "Sorry," he whispered.

A patch of brown appeared in the thicket, barely visible. It wasn't an animal; it was a shirt. A sombrero took shape, and the head under it.

Nate stroked the trigger.

A bandit shrieked and reared and collapsed, his sombrero flipping off as he sprawled flat.

"Then there were three," Fester said.

Nate reached for his powder horn when suddenly the woods rocked to gun blasts. Grabbing hold of Fester, he dived flat.

Above them lead sizzled.

"That was close," Fester breathed. "They know where we are."

"Stick with me," Nate said, and went to crawl into cover.

"Maybe we should split up," Fester suggested. "I go one way and you go another and we catch them between us."

"I have a better idea," Nate said. "We'll let them come to us."

"Are you sure that's smart?"

Nate moved to a pine and patted the ground next to him. "Lay right here."

Fester complied, whispering, "I hope to heaven you know what you're doin'."

Digging his fingers into the carpet of pine needles, Nate spread them over Fester's back.

"What in blazes?"

"You do the same to me," Nate directed. "Quickly. As many as you can reach."

Fester grabbed a handful. "Oh. I get it." He indulged in a quiet laugh.

They were covered from their necks to their knees when Nate motioned for the old man to be still.

A bandit was slinking in their direction but didn't see them for their camouflage.

Nate recognized the man Fester had shot in the shoulder. He fixed a bead, and when he was sure, put a slug in the bandit's brainpan.

Fester chortled much too loudly. "Damn, you're a hellion. Now it's two against two."

Some instinct, some inner sense, made Nate glance over his shoulder. "Look out!" he cried, and rolled just as Pedro and Sabino cut loose with pistols. Letting go of the Hawken, he clawed at his own. A slug tore into the ground next to him. Another clipped his whangs. He fired at Pedro's face but Pedro moved and the heavy ball struck his neck. Pedro stopped as if he had run into a wall and blood sprayed in a mist.

Fester got off a shot.

So did Sabino.

Nate aimed his second pistol, thumbed back the hammer, and squeezed.

Sabino acquired a third eye. He took a step, groaned, and buckled.

"We did it," Nate said, elated.

Fester didn't answer.

Turning, Nate said, "No." Rising to his knees, he clasped the old man's good hand. "Sabino?"

"Thrack," Fester said, and blood trickled from both corners of his mouth. "Back in the clearing."

"Why didn't you say something?"

Fester coughed, and now blood oozed from his nose. "Do me a favor, will you?"

"Anything," Nate said.

"Take care of Marabell."

"For as long as she lives," Nate promised.

"I hate to die lookin' like a chicken," Fester said. "Life is plumb ridiculous at times." He smiled, and was gone.

CHAPTER FORTY-FIVE

The dead warrior had a tomahawk. He was lying partly on top of it, and Winona didn't notice it at first. When she did, she rolled the body over and hefted it. "This will do nicely."

"A gun would be better," Bright Rainbow said.

"Not for what I have in mind. Keep watch for the Bloods."

Leaning her Hawken against the boulder, Winona began chopping the grass. She worked swiftly, methodically. Every second counted.

Sacripant heard the chopping. "What are you doing, woman?" he called out.

Winona didn't answer.

"What is that sound?"

"Come and see so I can put a ball into you," Winona taunted. Soon she had cleared a horseshoe shaped space about six feet across. It wasn't a lot but now Sacripant and Three Bulls couldn't sneak right up on them as the other warrior had done. She retreated to the boulder, dropped the tomahawk, and reclaimed her Hawken.

"Will it be soon, you think?" Bright Rainbow asked.

"There's no telling," Winona said.

Minutes crawled and nothing happened.

"What are they waiting for?" Bright Rainbow nervously wondered.

Winona thought she knew. "For their friends to catch up."

"When will that be?"

"There's no telling," Winona said again.

"Maybe we should slip away," Bright Rainbow proposed.

"They would jump us in the grass," Winona said. "This is as good a spot as any to make a stand."

Bright Rainbow looked at her. "You would make a good warrior."

Placing a hand on her shoulder, Winona smiled, and suddenly saw her eyes widen.

"Look out!"

Winona whirled, wondering if it was the voyageur or the Blood. It was both.

Winona jerked the Hawken up but Sacripant swatted the barrel before she could shoot and Three Bears slammed into her, smashing her against the boulder and seizing her wrists. In the blink of an eye she was pinned and helpless.

Sacripant leered and wrenched the Hawken from her grasp. "That was easier than I thought it would be."

Three Bulls growled in the Blood tongue.

"He says, *mon cherie*," Sacripant translated, "that for what you have done, you will take a long time dying, and suffer much."

Winona glared in defiance. She refused to show the dismay that filled her. She wouldn't give them the satisfaction.

Suddenly there was the blast of a shot. Three Bulls grunted and let go of Winona and staggered against Sacripant. They both stared in surprise at a hole in his buckskin shirt.

Winona was as stunned as they were.

There stood Bright Rainbow, the smoking flintlock in her hands, her young face as grimly set as an Apache's.

Three Bulls tried to speak but his legs folded. High on his neck was the exit wound. The ball had torn clear up through his chest before bursting out.

Sacripant let out a cry of rage, and attacked. He clubbed Bright Rainbow with the stock of his rifle and down she went.

Winona tried to unlimber a flintlock but he spun and rammed his rifle into her gut. The pain doubled her over. Seizing her, he hooked his foot behind her leg and flung her bodily to the ground.

"You and the flea both die, now!"

Winona feared he was right. She couldn't catch her breath, couldn't use a weapon.

Sacripant did a surprising thing; he cast his rifle aside. Then, jumping high into the air, he bent his knees.

Too late, Winona tried to roll away. He came down hard on her belly and her whole body exploded with agony. For a few seconds the world blurred. Then her vision cleared and Sacripant was straddling her, his hands around her throat.

"I will enjoy this, sweet one," Sacripant said, his face contorted with the violence of his bloodlust. His hands tightened, his fingers digging deeper.

Winona couldn't breathe. She bucked and she clawed at his hands but they were iron clamps. She tried to scratch his eyes but he jerked his head back. She kneed him but it had no effect. She swung a fist at his throat but he blocked the blow with his shoulder. She grabbed for her knife but couldn't reach it no matter how she strained.

Her lungs were close to bursting and she was close to passing out.

"Such a waste," Sacripant said. He was staring at her breasts.

Winona's vision was fading but she clearly saw the tomahawk slice into Sacripant's temple and crimson spray every which way.

Sacripant glanced up, startled, and the tomahawk bit into him again, in the throat. More blood spurted, spraying Winona. With an oath he heaved up off her and staggered back, pressing his hands to his pumping wounds.

"Not by you!" he gurgled at his slayer, and red froth bubbled from his mouth. He took a faltering step and died on his feet.

His body hit with a thud.

Struggling to breathe, Winona sat up.

Bright Rainbow held the bloody tomahawk in her small hands. Red drops dribbled down her forehead and her face was spattered with scarlet. She stared at Sacripant in shock.

"Come here, little one," Winona said, and gently pulled Bright Rainbow to her.

The tomahawk fell and Bright Rainbow's arms were around her and she began to cry in great racking sobs that shook her spare frame.

Winona held her and rocked her while around them the grass swayed in the soft breeze and a bird sang, and the scent of fresh blood filled the air.

EPILOGUE

It was early in the evening two days later and they were seated at a fire, roasting a rabbit Winona had shot. Hooves drummed and out of the woods galloped a black horse lathered with sweat.

Nate was out of the saddle before the bay stopped. He ran to Winona and they embraced, and he had never been so thankful for anything as to find her alive and unharmed. "Thank you, God," he said hoarsely.

"Took you long enough," Winona said, her own voice strained.

"Long story." Nate kissed her and looked into the loveliest eyes in all the world. "Sacripant?"

"Dead."

"Good riddance," Nate said, and looked about them. "Three Bulls?"

"Dead."

"The rest of the Bloods?"

"I shot one of them. The others are on their way back to their village, I would imagine."

Nate hugged her anew and inhaled the scent of her hair. "I can't wait to get home." He stepped back and smiled at Bright Rainbow. "And how about you? Are you ready to be taken to your people?"

"No," Winona said.

Nate had seldom been so surprised in his life. "No?"

Winona moved to Bright Rainbow and Bright Rainbow stood and put her arm around Winona's waist. "Husband," Winona said, and kissed the top of her head. "I would like you to meet our new daughter."

Nate stared at Winona and then at the girl and then at Winona again. "Well," he said.

"Is it all right?" Bright Rainbow anxiously asked. "Do you want me?"

Nate King squatted and held out his hand and smiled. "Welcome to the family."

FINI

MORE GREAT READS BY DAVID ROBBINS

ENDWORLD 28
DARK DAYS

The science fiction series that sweeps readers into a terrifyingApocalyptic future continues. The Warriors of Alpha Triad face their greatest threat yet. Their survivalist compound, the Home, has been invaded. Not by an enemy army. Not by the horrifying mutates. This time a shapeshifter is loose among the Family. Able to change into any of them at will, it is killing like there is no tomorrow.

BLOOD FEUD
HOUNDS OF HATE

Chace and Cassie Shannon are back. The feud between the Harkeys and the Shannons takes the twins from the hills of Arkansas to New Orleans, where Chace has a grand scheme to set them up in style. But if the Harkeys have anything to say about it, they'll be planted six feet under.

HIT RADIO

Franco Scarvetti has a problem. His psycho son has whacked a made man. Now a rival Family is out to do the same to his son. So Big Frank comes up with a plan. He sends his lethal pride and joy to run a radio station in a small town while he tries to smooth things over. But Big Frank never read Shakespeare and he forgets that a psycho by any other name is still.......a psycho.

THE WERELING

The original Horror classic is back. Ocean City has a lot going for it. Nice beaches. The boardwalk. Tourists. But something new is prowling Ocean City. Something that feasts on those tourists. Something that howls at the moon, and bullets can't stop. The Jersey Shore werewolf is loose.

ANGEL U
LET THERE BE LIGHT

Armageddon is a generation away, and the forces of light and darkness are preparing to clash in the ultimate battle. To prepare humankind, the angels establish a university of literal higher learning here on Earth.

A young man and a young woman meet, and begin to fall in love. Only to be caught up in demonic warfare when living evil seeks to destroy Angel U at all costs.

A GIRL, THE END OF THE WORLD AND EVERYTHING

Courtney Hewitt lived a perfectly ordinary life. She had her mom and dad and brother and sister and some friends and a boy she liked. School mostly bored her but they made her go, so hey. Then global war broke out and several countries let fly with nuclear missiles and biological and chemical weapons. Suddenly her life was no longer ordinary. Now Courtney has radiation and mutations to deal with. To say nothing of the not-so-dead who eat the living. A lot of people might give up in despair. Not Courtney. When the going gets tough, the tough kick butt.

Made in the USA
Middletown, DE
16 December 2014